Solomon Smee Versus the Monkeys

Joanna Nadin is the author of *Maisie Morris and the Awful Arkwrights*. *Solomon Smee Versus the Monkeys* is her second book. She says of it, "Solomon Smee looks just like my little brother James who wore spectacles and had dark, dark hair that stood out in many directions at once – all of them wrong. But, unlike Solomon, James did not have a nasty aunt in a hat like a dismembered raven, and a jolly good thing too. Oh, and the coconuts and satsumas trick was a special secret that a nice vicar told my best friend Helen, who then told me, and now I'm passing it on to you, in case you ever need to catch a monkey." Joanna's previous jobs include working as a lifeguard, radio newsreader and wardrobe assistant – during which she washed the underpants of many famous people. She is now a political writer and adviser in government. She lives in Peckham, London.

By the same author

Maisie Morris and the Awful Arkwrights

Solomon Smee Versus the Monkeys

Joanna Nadin

illustrated by Arthur Robins

WALKER BOOKS
AND SUBSIDIARIES
LONDON · BOSTON · SYDNEY · AUCKLAND

First published 2004 by Walker Books Ltd
87 Vauxhall Walk, London SE11 5HJ

2 4 6 8 10 9 7 5 3

Text © 2004 Joanna Nadin
Illustrations © 2004 Arthur Robins

The right of Joanna Nadin and Arthur Robins to be identified as
author and illustrator respectively of this work has been asserted by
them in accordance with the Copyright, Designs and Patents Act 1988

This book has been typeset in Randumhouse and Shinn Light

Printed in Great Britain by Cox & Wyman Ltd, Reading, Berkshire

British Library Cataloguing in Publication Data:
a catalogue record for this book
is available from the British Library

ISBN 1-84428-626-6

www.walkerbooks.co.uk

For Giles

Contents

So Many Monkeys

What a lot of monkeys there are!

There are monkeys with long bulbous noses that can sniff out a ripe plum across a mile of mountain.

There are monkeys with a single spindly finger for digging weevils out of tricky places.

There are monkeys as small as bats with orange tufty ears and others as big as bears with luxurious long hair that you could plait if they sat still long enough.

There are monkeys with white faces and even monkeys with blue bottoms.

There are enormous apes, bad-tempered baboons and leaping lemurs that can jump as high as elephants. There are marmosets, tamarinds, gibbons, gorillas and orang-utans.

But some of the most interesting monkeys of all are the ordinary kind. Not too big and not too small.

No tufts, no colourful bottoms and very unim-pressive noses. Just short brown fur, long tails and eyes like black buttons.

But they are just the sort of monkey that can cause all manner of mischief and bother, as the small town of Royal Nerdal Norton was about to find out.

Royal Nerdal Norton

In the Kingdom of Elsewhere, just to the left of Nomansland and not far from Xanadu, sat Royal Nerdal Norton – a town so small and insignificant that only the gods and mapmakers had heard of it.

It was not a particularly special sort of place. It had a chemist shop which was run by Mr Bottleopener. Next door to that was the Almighty Honk Car Repair and Accessories Centre, where Mr Ganges the mechanic fixed all the bicycles, buses, scooters and cars of Royal Nerdal Norton.

On the corner of the main square was the great, grey, creaky-looking Limpopo and Limpopo department store, run by Mr Limpopo senior and his son, Mr Limpopo junior. And opposite that were the Municipal Offices, where council clerks sat on three floors busily attending to the many Municipal problems. There was an office where you could pay your bills and another where you could claim your benefits. There was an office for reporting stray-dog droppings and another for reporting stray dogs. There was one for painting yellow lines on the side of the road and one for removing them again. In fact, there was an office for every eventuality imaginable – and some unimaginable besides.

Except for the occasional invasion by pirates from the North or bandits from the South, nothing much happened in Royal Nerdal Norton until one hot and sticky summer not too long ago.

It was so hot that the milk from the cows curdled before it even reached the bottles, leaving Mr Jambutty the ice-cream-monger temporarily out of business.

It was so hot that the tar on the roads melted and everyone trailed black, sticky shoe marks all over rugs and floors behind them – keeping the Royal Nerdal Norton Kwik-Klene Carpet Shampoo company on 24-hour alert.

The heat made the make-up on the Benevolent Society of Ladies' faces run down in rivers of waxy pink and blue, and their enormous hairdos wilt. The once crisp and smart khaki uniforms of the army were sweaty and damp and they had long since stopped fighting because it was so hot that no one had bothered to invade for a month.

It was so hot at night that Mr Ganges the mechanic had abandoned his duvet (and Mrs Ganges) and had taken to sleeping on the roof. It was so hot that even the crickets and cockroaches stopped chirruping, and the only sound was the loud ticking of the clock on the Municipal Offices of Royal Nerdal Norton, counting down the minutes until sunrise.

But in a small house on the wrong side of town, past the Arthur Gomez Memorial Bandstand, past the Barry Chatterjee Centre for Unruly Youth and towards the outskirts of town, where the wide brown river flowed slowly to the sea, a single light bulb burned late into the night. Solomon Smee, a small boy with brown-rimmed glasses and dark, dark hair, had things on his mind.

Solomon Smee

Solomon Smee could not sleep. He had tried counting sheep, and when that failed he tried counting beetles because they were smaller and he thought they would tire him out quicker. But they kept running around in circles in his head and he ended up counting some twice, which just got confusing and made him even less sleepy.

In the end he gave up and thought about what was worrying him. There were two things that he listed in his head:

1. I am bored.
2. I want a new mum.

The first problem was simple to explain – it was the summer holidays and Solomon always got bored in the summer holidays because nothing remotely interesting ever happened. The second problem was more complicated and had subcategories, like:

2(b) I wish that Aunt Nehemiah would turn into a big meat pie and a dog would eat her for dinner.

Now I expect you have a couple of questions in your own mind now, such as:

Where is Solomon's own mum?

Just how horrible is Aunt Nehemiah?

And here are the answers.

Once upon a time Solomon had a super mother. She was called Barbara and she knew all about times tables and made biscuits with sprinkly bits on top and could sing all the words to several musicals. Solomon loved her very much. But one day she caught an incurable disease which was so new and unheard of that no one knew what to call it. They just said she had caught "it". First of all her ears shrivelled up, then her legs and arms inflated so she looked like someone had pumped her up with a bicycle pump. Then she stopped eating, and within a week she was dead.

So now Solomon lived with his dad, Harry, and his Aunt Nehemiah.

Mr Smee was a kind but quiet man who worked long hours for the Official Municipal Complaints Office but never once complained himself. He liked athletics and aeroplanes and he had the same spectacles and dark, dark hair as Solomon.

Aunt Nehemiah was Mr Smee's sister, but she was a different kettle of fish altogether. She had arrived to take charge of Solomon a month after his mother died. One morning Solomon opened the door and there she stood, with a black hat like a dismembered raven, a large leather trunk and a face like an undertaker.

She had once belonged to an order of pitiless and military nuns called the Sisters of No Mercy, but even they had found her too severe and joyless. She had a mean streak as wide as the Gravesend estuary and a hairy wart on her upper lip that quivered when she was angry – which was often.

First to go was the television, which she said would rot Solomon's brain. Then went the jams and jellies and sweet jar, which she said would rot his teeth. There was to be no more cricket, no hide-and-seek and no more betting on which fly would reach the top of the window first, because gambling, according to Aunt Nehemiah, was the work of the devil himself and as bad as thieving or cheating at exams.

Aunt Nehemiah was the reason Solomon wanted a new mum. Well, wouldn't you? Sometimes Solomon would pester his dad with suggestions of suitable ladies. "What about Mr Ganges' wife's sister Aurelia with the funny eye? Or Miss Haversage the vet's nurse who can hold a cow upside down with one hand?"

But as much as Solomon pleaded with his father, Aunt Nehemiah did her best to put an end to the idea.

"A new mother?" she snapped, her eyes glowering and her mood blacker than ink. "What do you need a new mother for? And besides," she would add, "there's no room unless you want to sleep in bunk beds with me."

Solomon did not want that, not one bit. Aunt Nehemiah snored like a walrus and smelt of mothballs.

And Mr Smee was no help. He would only shake his head and agree with Aunt Nehemiah. "Oh we do all right just the three of us, don't we? You're happy, aren't you?" he would say. And Solomon, not wanting to argue, would nod sadly.

But Solomon was not happy. He was not happy at all. Night after night he would lie in his small wooden bed, with its yellow candlewick cover, wondering what sort of new mum he would like. Would tall or short be better? With dark curls or long blonde floaty hair? Would he like the kind of mum who let him eat crisps and drink fizzy pop? Or one who made him sit up straight at the table and use napkins, and told him off for licking his knife?

He thought so hard about this that he almost forgot about his other complaint. But not for long. Because something was about to happen. Something so whopping that the whole of Royal Nerdal Norton would talk about it for years to come. Something so fantastical that Solomon would never complain about being bored again.

Because as Solomon lay awake worrying and the rest of Royal Nerdal Norton slumbered fatly, dreaming of baked Alaska and rain, sixty-seven monkeys padded softly into town.

They were small and brown and itching for exciting things to do.

Solomon and the Complaints Office

The next morning Solomon stared glumly at his breakfast and sighed.

"What's the matter with you?" snapped Aunt Nehemiah. "Eat that bloater up or you'll have it for tea. Waste not, want not."

Solomon poked the grey fish with his fork. It stared back with sullen glassy eyes and the look of something that had been dead for a very long time indeed.

Mr Smee sat quietly at the other end of the table, trying to ignore Aunt Nehemiah. He was reading the *Nerdal Norton Packet,* a gossipy newspaper whose front page was full of tales of heatwave-related catastrophes. "Mayor Declares Ice-Cream Crisis!" proclaimed the headline. And then in slightly smaller letters, "by our ace reporter Boyce Spink".

Solomon sighed again. "I'm bored," he

announced to no one in particular.

"Bored?" screeched Aunt Nehemiah. Then she said it again, even louder. "Bored? Why, in my day we would have been grateful to be bored. We were too busy being funnelled up chimneys to earn a living, with newspapers strapped to our feet instead of shoes and nothing but a cheese cracker for lunch."

Aunt Nehemiah said "in my day" a lot.

"There are plenty of things for you to do here, young man," said Aunt Nehemiah. "You can count all the lumps of coal in the coal cellar for a start. Then there's potatoes to peel, herrings to gut, and if you're very good I've got a bunion that needs scraping."

Solomon shuddered. Having to stay at home was what he had been afraid of. Nothing good or interesting ever happened with Aunt Nehemiah. In fact, bad things usually did.

Mr Smee, unable to ignore the kerfuffle any longer, put down his newspaper. "Er, I have an idea," he said cautiously. He was always cautious when talking to Aunt Nehemiah. "Why doesn't Solomon come to work with me this week?"

24

Solomon couldn't believe his ears. Nor could Aunt Nehemiah.

"Don't be absurd, Harry!" she exploded. "Take a small boy to the Council Offices? He'll just get in the way of Municipal business."

But Mr Smee had anticipated this. "I think it would be good for him to see what it's like to go to work all day. You're always saying how hard you worked up chimneys and down diamond mines when you were his age."

"Yes, yes!" agreed Solomon. "I'll be super good and learn how to file things and type and all sorts, Aunt."

Aunt Nehemiah glared at him.

"But there is one condition, Solomon," said Mr Smee. "If the Mayor comes in you'll have to hide in the wastepaper bin."

"That's OK!" said Solomon. Which it was. Because the wastepaper bin was quite large enough for Solomon. It was red, with a swing lid to push rubbish through which could serve as a viewing slot.

"You give in to him too easily, Harry, that's your trouble," said Aunt Nehemiah. "Spoilt, that boy is. Why, in my day we'd have been grateful to stay at

home with our aunts, peeling potatoes and counting coal. We weren't allowed to shilly-shally around
with our fathers. Oh no."

"In your day dinosaurs still roamed the earth,"
whispered Solomon to himself.

"What was that?" said Aunt Nehemiah.

"Nothing, Aunt," said Solomon. "Nothing at all."

And he smiled an invisible smile that only showed
on the inside.

Unusual Complaints

As you may or may not remember, depending on how well you have been concentrating so far, Mr Smee was the Official Complaints Clerk for the Royal Nerdal Norton Municipal Council. It was not a job that he loved. He did not leap out of bed with the sort of gusto I expect you have on a school morning. Once upon a time, when he was small, Mr Smee had dreamt of being a space explorer or a scientist or an elephant trainer. But his sister Nehemiah had told him to stop daydreaming and fiddle-faddling about and get a proper job with a desk and an office and paperclips. So he had.

He sat in a small hot room on the ground floor of the town hall, which he shared with his secretary, Mrs Britt-Dullforce, a large and enthusiastic woman with a bosom as big as two birthday balloons. She wore garish hairy outfits which she knitted herself from the wool of a herd of endangered sheep that lived in her backyard. As well as being a founder member of the Royal Nerdal Norton Vegetarian Brigade, she was also the Equal Opportunities Officer for the Benevolent Society of Ladies and head of the Monkey Protection League. Mr Smee found her slightly annoying and a bit scary and was jolly glad she was already married, in case Solomon got any funny ideas. Her job was to type up the complaints for Mr Smee to investigate.

Usually the complaints were about the heat, or noisy neighbours, or the hopeless Court Magician, Maurice Hankey. Things like: "It's so hot that my rubber flip-flops have stuck to the lino – will you please come and rescue me"; or "Will someone please tell Mrs Darjeeling at 23 Malabar Street to stop playing Johnny Sparkles records at five o'clock in the morning"; or "That wretched Court Magician Maurice has turned my husband into a goat again and he has eaten three chairs and a book about badgers".

But this morning the complaints were to be unusual. Very unusual indeed. Before Mr Smee had time to open his pencil case and lay his pens neatly on the desk, before Mrs Britt-Dullforce had time to check the Children at Work Act (Subsection C) to see whether Solomon was breaking any Municipal laws, and before Solomon had a chance to spin round on the twirly office chairs and make himself sick, Mr Ganges the mechanic from the Almighty Honk Car Repair and Accessories Centre came bursting through the door with his overalls skew-whiff and a wild look in his eyes. Solomon jumped straight into the wastepaper bin and peered out through the swing flap.

"Mr Ganges," said Mr Smee. "What on earth is the matter?"

"A 100 per cent tip-top emergency is the matter, Harry," he said, banging a sprocket on the table and leaving a rather large and oily dent. "You know me, Harry – I'm not one to complain." (This was not strictly true – Mr Ganges had notched up a whopping forty-seven complaints in the last year, most of them about Mrs Ganges.) "I am not one to complain, but yesterday evening a gang of criminals broke into my garage and attached the wrong parts to several vehicles. I now have a delivery van with a racing saddle and novelty bell and a bicycle with windscreen-wipers and a stereo system in the saddlebag. My thought is that a rival set-up is hoping to sabotage my business!"

Mr Smee was not at all convinced. Criminals were few and far between in Royal Nerdal Norton – the last time they had had any bother was when three of Barry Chatterjee's unruly boys had got out and stolen a carton of rum 'n' rhubarb ice cream from Mr Jambutty.

"Have you checked with Barry Chatterjee?" asked Mr Smee. "Maybe some of the boys got loose overnight."

"Tied to their beds with parcel string," said Mr Ganges. "Every last one of them."

"Hmm," said Mr Smee. "This is a difficult one."

"I expect it's pensioners protesting about the cost of bus passes," said Mrs Britt-Dullforce, typing frantically to keep up with Mr Ganges.

"Impossible," said Mr Ganges. "The door was locked and the window is ten feet up and only one foot square. That's far too high and small for a pensioner with a gammy hip and whatnot else they're always complaining about. No, it's a rival gang with an exceptionally small accomplice. Maybe one of those trained magpies. Or an armed elf. They're tricky little things, elves, you know – always up to no good."

"Elves aren't real, Mr Ganges," piped up Solomon from the wastepaper bin.

"Oh hello, Solomon young man, I didn't see you down there," said Mr Ganges – who liked Solomon, as he was a polite boy. "And of course elves are real. Otherwise who would the leprechauns play with?"

"Are there any other clues, Mr Ganges?" asked Mr Smee, trying to end the rather pointless discussion.

But he was interrupted by the arrival of Mrs Perambulator and her twin daughters, Maureen and Doreen.

Mrs Perambulator was a loud woman with a lot of money, a wild imagination and precious little common sense. She spoilt her daughters rotten and as a result they were an obnoxious pair. They never ate their greens, never did their homework and were allowed to wear high heels even though they were only eight.

"Mr Smee, this is a catastrophe of the first order!" shrieked Mrs Perambulator. "Hairy men on scooters rode right up to my house and tried to terrorize me and my precious poppets and then posted my poor parrot Colin through next door's letterbox."

Maureen and Doreen nodded furiously while sucking on sherry trifle flavoured popsicles (which they were allowed to eat whenever they wanted, even for breakfast).

Solomon, annoyed at Maureen and Doreen, groaned from inside the bin, making it echo ominously.

"Aaagh!" wailed Mrs Perambulator. "You've one of them in here! Get an axe and a long pointy stick."

Maureen and Doreen clutched each other in fright.

"Quick, girls!" said Mrs Perambulator. "Outside at once. Nowhere is safe!" And they bolted out the door.

Mr Smee sighed. "Solomon, try to keep quiet and not scare people or I'll have no choice but to send you back home to Aunt Nehemiah."

Solomon decided to do as he was told.

Next in line was Mr Jambutty, the out-of-work ice-cream vendor. "Mr Smee, it is terrible!" he said. "I was asleep happily inside my cart when a league of undersized spacemen descended from the outer cosmos and dropped a flowerpot on my head. Awful they were, small and dangerous and armed with nails made of aluminium. I am most upset."

"Are you sure?" asked Mr Smee.

"Absolutely, sir," said Mr Jambutty.

Mr Smee shook his head. In all his years as Official Complaints Clerk he had never heard the like of this before.

"There's only one thing for it," he said. "I'll have to call the Mayor." And he picked up a bright red phone, marked EMERGENCY.

Mayor Plusfour was asleep at his desk, dreaming of film stars and raspberry meringues, when the phone rang.

He was a red-faced man with a long waxed moustache and a short temper. He did not suffer fools (or anyone else for that matter) gladly, and he especially did not like to be woken up when he was dreaming of raspberry meringues.

"Who is this?" he demanded in an annoyed voice. "Smee, eh? Well, what do you want? ... Aliens and saboteurs? This is nonsense, Smee. I'm coming down at once to give you what for!" And he slammed down the phone, stamped out of his gilt-lined office (complete with mini Jacuzzi and portable bar) down the corridor, right at the Office for Traffic Jam Control, past the Department for Dog Dropping Removal, past Mr Jambutty and Mr Ganges and straight into Mr Smee's office.

"What in the name of Saint Strangeways is going on?" he demanded.

"Oh it's terrible, Mayor!" said Mr Jambutty, peering round the door. "Hideous gangs of interplanetary thieves are ransacking every house in Royal Nerdal Norton!"

"Don't be ridiculous," said the Mayor, who was clearly in one of his "not standing for any nonsense" moods. "It is obviously this infernal heat making everyone doolally. I have never heard such a far-fetched load of codswallop. Tell them to go home and take a cold shower and stop watching so much television. It's giving them ideas."

This was a bit rich coming from the Mayor, who liked nothing better than an afternoon of television. He loved crime programmes where good-looking young detectives in sunglasses solved fiendishly difficult plots using only their wits, a Swiss army knife and a vast array of computers. Best of all he loved soap operas, with their exotic locations, impossibly beautiful heroines and catchy theme tunes.

Meanwhile, in the wastepaper bin, trouble was brewing.

Solomon needed to cough. The trouble with needing to cough and not being able to is that the harder you try not to cough, the more tickly your throat becomes. And the more tickly your throat becomes, the more you need to cough. Which Solomon eventually did – an almighty hack that rattled the bin lid.

"What was that?" said the Mayor.

"What was what?" said Mr Smee nervously.

"That noise. I distinctly heard something."

Mr Smee looked at the bin.

"Talking rubbish," he said triumphantly. "It was Mrs Britt-Dullforce talking rubbish again."

"What?" said Mrs Britt-Dullforce.

"Mmm, well just see that she stops it," said the Mayor. And off he thundered again, past Mr Jambutty and Mr Ganges, past the Department for Dog Dropping Removal, left at the Office for Traffic Jam Control and into his own office, where he poured himself a large Strawberry Sunrise.

Solomon was so excited by everything that had happened he thought he might very well explode. But he was also a sensible boy, and he knew it couldn't be aliens, or giants with razors for fingers riding motorbikes. So if it wasn't them, then who was it?

NOW SHOWING

The Story of Lysandra

"Midgets," said Aunt Nehemiah that afternoon when Mr Smee and Solomon got home. "That's what's behind all this, mark my words, Harry. I don't like them – all small and sneaky. You should round them all up and put them in cages and then post them somewhere very cold and dark." She clattered plates of suspicious grey meat down on the table. "Now eat your liver before it gets cold, Solomon," she added. "And then you can wash up, mop the kitchen floor and polish the doorknobs – all thirty-three of them."

Solomon scowled and chewed on some gristle.

That night, after washing up the greasy grey dinner plates, mopping the kitchen floor and pol-ishing all thirty-three doorknobs, Solomon lay in bed with Mr Smee sitting on the edge and they talked about all that had happened that day. There was a lot to go over. Who was behind all the mayhem? Was it bandits? Or was it just the heat? It certainly was hot at the moment – why, you could fry an egg on the iron roof of the outhouse if you got the angle right. There was another question playing on Solomon's mind as well.

"Why is the Mayor so angry all the time?" he asked.

Mr Smee tucked the sheets around Solomon and smiled down at his big brown eyes and dark, dark hair. "It's quite a long story. Are you sure you can stay awake?"

"Oh yes, of course!" said Solomon.

"Very well," said his dad. "This is the story of how the Mayor lost his happiness.

"The Mayor wasn't always a big angry shouty man, you know. Once upon a time, when I was a little boy – about your age – he was a slim, athletic and dashing sort of chap with an elegant moustache, two swimming trophies and a medal for good conduct from the Royal Naval Academy of Nerdal Norton. He was married to a lovely lady called Meribel who was kind to old people and sick animals and sang songs of distant lands which made everyone smile to hear her.

"When their daughter Lysandra was born they thought they were the happiest, luckiest people alive. Lysandra was the most beautiful girl in the Kingdom of Elsewhere. Everyone who saw her said she must have been carried down from the heavens by flights of angels."

"Yuck!" said Solomon.

Mr Smee laughed. "I know, but she really was that amazing. Anyway, because our surnames were so close together in the alphabet and there were no Qs or Rs – not after Sidney Quick got complications from chickenpox – we sat next to each other at school. And we became the best of friends. We would go swimming together and play at each other's houses."

"You used to play at the Mayor's house?" gasped Solomon, who had never been allowed to play anywhere but the backyard. "Wow, what was it like?"

"It was a big pink mansion on the right side of town, with pillars and an ornamental sunken garden at the back. It was decorated with the finest flock velvet wallpaper and soft swirly carpets. There were crystal chandeliers and brass doorknobs and a stuffed tiger's head in the hallway on a wooden plaque which read, 'Cowpatty Province, August 1893'. And before you ask, I have no idea what that means.

"Best of all, the Mayor had an enormous library with books from all over the world. Lysandra and I would spend hours in there, reading about space explorers and wild cowboys and—"

"Yes, but what happened next?" said Solomon impatiently.

"OK, OK, to cut a long story short, before Lysandra was even eight years old, tragedy struck. Her mother – Meribel – disappeared."

"What do you mean, disappeared?" asked Solomon.

"Exactly that," said Mr Smee. "One minute she was enjoying a night out at the Lux cinema with the old Court Magician, Percy Spandex, and the next, according to Percy, she was gone in a puff of smoke and a smell of burnt pilchards. For several months afterwards the Mayor and Lysandra searched the cinema every night after closing time, but all they found were a pair of socks and a packet of wine gums."

"But couldn't Percy just magic her back again?" asked Solomon.

"He tried," said Mr Smee. "But all he could conjure up was a Swedish milkmaid called Ulrika and then a very pretty but rather selfish heiress called Tara. The Mayor and Lysandra hated both of them. Meribel was unique and irreplaceable, you see."

"Like my mum," said Solomon sadly.

"That's right," said Mr Smee, ruffling Solomon's hair. "So to punish Percy the Mayor sacked him and sent him off to the Forest of Certain Death to hunt for the Hooded Quangle."

"But the Hooded Quangle doesn't exist, Dad," said Solomon.

"Exactly," said Mr Smee. "No one ever saw Percy again. Instead the Mayor hired Maurice Hankey, who is quite definitely the worst court magician Royal Nerdal Norton has even seen."

"But what about the Mayor?" asked Solomon, wishing his dad would get to the point.

"OK, OK, I'm just coming to that bit," said Mr Smee. "Over the years the Mayor stopped being a lithe, dashing sportsman with a heart of gold and legs like steel and became more and more miserable. He snapped at everyone and became as mean and ugly in his looks as in his thoughts. Worst of all, the Mayor didn't like Lysandra to leave the house for fear of her getting lost or stolen or disappearing in a puff of smoke like her mum. So to keep her father happy she stayed inside and read and knitted with nothing but the Mayor and all the books in the library for company."

"But didn't you still play there?" asked Solomon.

"No," said Mr Smee, shaking his head sadly. "No. Every day I would ring the doorbell, and every day the Mayor would send me away again with an earful of shouting and a sinking feeling in my tummy. Every day for another ten years until I left school. And then, well, I met your mother and I suppose I had other things to think about. But I've never forgotten Lysandra."

"But what happened to her? Did she turn as mean as the Mayor? Or did she get married too?" said Solomon, who was full of questions.

"Well, Lysandra grew up nicely regardless. She was as kind as her mother and loved animals and birds and was the light of the Mayor's life – though he would never admit it. She danced and sang and never once grumbled, because she loved her father very much and didn't want to upset him as he

46

had had quite enough upset already. And because she spent so long in the library she was fantastically clever and could speak French and Mandarin and name an animal beginning with 'N', which I bet you can't."

Solomon thought for a minute. Dad was right. He couldn't!

Mr Smee continued. "The same year as I met your mum, when Lysandra turned eighteen too, suitors began to call at the house, some urged on by memories of long ago and others by rumours of a girl so pretty it would make the gods themselves weep with joy to see her. But the Mayor did not want Lysandra to go, so instead of letting her marry whomever she chose, he would send them all away. One by one, all the suitors gave up, and so as far as I know, Lysandra is still somewhere in the Mayor's house, all alone but for her books. And that is how the Mayor became a bothersome shouty sort of person."

Mr Smee had a sad, faraway look in his eyes.

"Are you OK, Dad?" asked Solomon.

"Of course," said Mr Smee, shaking himself to and smiling quickly. "That's enough stories for one night.

It's time for bed. You must be sleepy, and we've got work again in the morning." He gave Solomon a hug and then pulled the switch to turn off the single light bulb. "Goodnight, son."

"Goodnight, Dad."

But Solomon wasn't sleepy. In fact, he was very excited. Lysandra, he thought to himself. She was the one for his dad, he knew it. But getting them to meet again was going to be trickier than three bunches of monkeys.

More Complaints

The next day Mr Smee sat at his Municipal desk in his smart but sweaty Municipal suit and sighed a big, Municipal sort of sigh. Solomon sat next to him in the wastepaper bin and sighed as well. All was most definitely not well in Royal Nerdal Norton. They had already logged eight complaints and it was still only 11 o'clock in the morning. Whatever it was had not gone away at all but was bigger and badder than ever.

First in line that morning was Mr Bottleopener the chemist. "Mr Smee," he said. "I have been pillaged by pygmies with a taste for laxatives and haemorrhoid cream. There must be a gang of very sore-bottomed thieves out there somewhere, and I demand they be captured at once."

Next was Manjit the postman, who said a fiend had inserted his radio down the toilet and every time he flushed he could hear a gurgly selection of popular jazz medleys.

On top of these disasters, Mr Limpopo junior from Limpopo and Limpopo department store had had two dozen bananas and a caramel custard stolen from his fridge and eaten very messily on his prize settee. Two corporals in the army barracks claimed that their elephant tranquillizer guns had been stolen, and that several colleagues were now stunned and guaranteed to sleep for a week. The Benevolent Society of Ladies had had to abandon its choir practice after a spate of eerie hooping noises in the rafters. And the list of missing items had grown to include one pair of Razzmatazz roller boots, a Victoria sponge, two Cs and an E-flat key from a baby grand piano and a picture of someone's aunt in a hat made of fruit.

To cap it all, the *Nerdal Norton Packet* was full of news of yesterday's strange events.

"Spacemen stole my parrot!" was splashed across the front page.

After lodging her complaint with Mr Smee, Mrs Perambulator, along with Maureen and Doreen, had gone straight round to the newspaper offices to see

Chief Reporter Boyce Spink. Boyce Spink was a sneaky sort who wore an old macintosh and carried a little tape recorder everywhere he went. You never could be sure if something you accidentally said one morning in the butcher's queue would not be front page news the next day. He was a master of exaggeration, embellishment and downright lies. Today's story was no exception.

"Slim and stunning single mum, Petunia Perambulator, 29, says she and her award-winning daughters have been terrorized by a gang of hairy-faced pirates carrying cutlasses and singing demonic sea shanties," read the copy. "'I was terrified!' said Mrs Perambulator, former Miss Teen Nerdal Norton. 'My life flashed before my eyes.'"

There was a picture of Mrs Perambulator with an enormous hairdo, her hand covering her mouth as if to look aghast with horror. Maureen and Doreen were sat either side of her in matching dresses, clutching toy ponies and eating ice creams.

Underneath was a little box with more writing in it. "Things going 'bump' in the night? Aliens in your outside lavatory? Thieves, bandits or just plain old baddies?" it read. "Call Boyce Spink on Nerdal

Norton 5555. Fifty rupees for every story we print."

"Slim?" snorted Mr Smee. "She's as wide as a hippopotamus and about as intelligent. And if she's twenty-nine then I'm a monkey's uncle." And he pushed the paper into the bin.

"Ow!" said Solomon.

"Sorry, I forgot," said Mr Smee.

But the problems were not over yet. The Mayor stormed into Mr Smee's office, his face very red and his moustache particularly bushy.

"Smee, I want words. That half-bit hack Boyce Spink has been on the phone accusing me of all manner of Municipal failures. He claims he has an exclusive tip-off from someone within these very walls that we believe this to be the work of the notorious criminals the Nutmeg Gang.

"Who are the Nutmeg Gang?" asked Mrs Britt-Dullforce.

"They're a band of ruthless escaped convicts from Xanadu. Their trademark is that they leave a calling card scented with nutmeg wherever they go."

"Well there you go, then, it can't be them," said Mrs Britt-Dullforce. "There's no nutmeg smell round here."

"No, just something very fishy," said Mr Smee.

"Well of course it isn't them!" retorted the Mayor angrily. "Because this is all cooked up in people's overactive imaginations by the heatwave and is not being helped by Spink, who is feeding them ideas in order to sell his papers."

"Oh, Mayor," said Mrs Britt-Dullforce. "I don't think anyone would do something that naughty, would they? I mean – that's lying."

"Exactly," said the Mayor. "I want you to put an end to this gossip and tittle-tattle immediately or you'll both be demoted to the Office for Naming New Streets."

And he stamped off for a long sherry and cola with double cherries.

Solomon stuck his head up out of the bin. "Call Boyce Spink!" he said. "And tell him the truth."

"But we don't know what the truth is," said Mr Smee.

"Well we can just tell him that what he's said so far couldn't be further from it," said Solomon.

"OK," said Mr Smee. "Anyway, I don't think we have any choice." And he picked up the other phone, which was not marked "EMERGENCY" but which was brown and rather dull in comparison, and called Nerdal Norton 5555.

Boyce Spink was delighted. An exclusive interview with the very man at the heart of the matter would sell his paper like hot cakes. He came over to the Municipal Council Offices at once, in his macintosh and with a smile like an alligator.

"So, Mr Smee – or can I call you Harry?" he began, flicking the switch on his tape recorder and sitting on Mr Smee's desk.

"Er, I suppose so," said Mr Smee.

"So, Harry, this must all be very exciting for a man like you. I mean, you seem a dynamic kind of guy, someone who really takes charge in a sticky situation."

Mr Smee had never thought of himself as dynamic before. But in a way, he supposed, he was in charge. Gosh, he thought to himself. Which was the worst thing he could have thought and exactly what Boyce Spink wanted him to think.

"So, Harry, tell me, who exactly is behind all the goings-on?"

"Well I don't really know, to be honest. No one does. Not even the Mayor. I mean – he thinks it's just

56

people getting hot and bothered in this heatwave and making things up," said Mr Smee, quite fired up from Boyce Spink's flattery.

Unfortunately, despite what your mother or father may tell you, there are some situations where honesty is the very worst policy. Talking to newspaper reporters is one of these. In fact, if one ever asks you a question you must say "no comment". Or you could end up in some very hot water indeed.

Despite being only eight years old and inside a wastepaper bin, Solomon knew this was one of those cases and shook his head. This was not good. Not good at all.

"Interesting, interesting," said Boyce Spink, smiling.

"Well some people have been saying it's aliens, but why would aliens come here anyway?" said Mr Smee.

"Maybe they're planning to take over the town?" prompted Boyce Spink.

"But why would they do that?" asked Mr Smee.

"Perhaps we're sitting on a diamond mine," suggested Boyce Spink. "And, well – do you have any evidence that proves they are not aliens?"

"Well not exactly," said Mr Smee. "Although why

would they steal tranquillizer guns? Wouldn't they have supernova stun guns or something already?"

"So they've struck again – and are now armed and dangerous?" said Boyce Spink.

"Well, I..." began Mr Smee, wondering how he had been so stupid as to let that cat out of the bag.

"And instead of being honest with the public, who have a right to know that there are aliens wandering round town with huge guns and missiles and who knows what else, the Mayor is trying to tell them that nothing is happening at all?"

"Um, well, I wouldn't put it quite like that..." said Mr Smee, thinking that this was not what he had had in mind for putting the record straight.

"Hmm," said Mr Spink. "This doesn't look good."

He was right. It didn't. There was no doubt about it. Mr Smee had made a colossal mistake and the Mayor was bound to find out.

The Newspaper Story

"Council in Catastrophe Cover-up!" ran the headline on the *Nerdal Norton Packet* the next morning.

But that wasn't the worst of it. The story underneath was just as Solomon had feared.

"Mild-mannered Complaints Officer Harry Smee admits that he hasn't a clue and neither has Mayor Plusfour..." read Solomon aloud at the breakfast table. "Tragic single father Mr Haroon Smee, 34, says aliens with stolen guns could be hiding under your stairs at this very moment, waiting to drill for diamonds in your rockery."

"What's so tragic about me?" asked Mr Smee.

Solomon ignored him and continued. "In an exclusive interview with me, your ace reporter Boyce Spink, Mr Smee admitted that the council doesn't know what to do about the problem. And in a shocking revelation he told me that this is only being made worse by obstruction from the Mayor himself, who does not want to reveal the truth about the danger."

"But I didn't say that!" protested Mr Smee. "He made it up and now he's twisting it to make me sound foolish."

"I could have told you this would happen," said Aunt Nehemiah as she slapped a pair of withered kippers onto his plate. "Never trust a newspaper man."

"But it's not Dad's fault," said Solomon. "He didn't mean to make it sound so bad."

"In my day," retorted Aunt Nehemiah, "small children were seen and not heard. Now eat that up or you'll get it cold for pudding tonight."

Solomon stared gloomily at his plate. Why couldn't he have toast or cereal for breakfast, like normal children?

At the office the situation was even worse. There was a queue stretching right out of the waiting-room of the Official Municipal Complaints Office, past the Department for Dog Dropping Removal, left at the Office for Traffic Jam Control and all the way to the Mayor's own gilt-lined office with its mini Jacuzzi and portable lounge bar.

Overnight, the menace, whatever it was, had stolen and drunk a consignment of whisky from the Pay-A-Bit-Less supermarket. They had then hijacked the town bus and driven it the wrong way up the High Street before crashing it into Mr Jambutty's temporarily out-of-action mobile ice-cream wagon, making it permanently out of action.

"It's no use," said Mr Smee. "I'll have to call the Mayor again. Though what he'll say after that newspaper article, I do not want to find out."

Mr Smee picked up the phone marked EMERGENCY. "That's odd," he said. There was no buzzing tone. He rattled it, but it stayed stubbornly silent.

Someone who never stayed stubbornly silent, however, was Mayor Plusfour, who, angered by the morning newspaper and by the horrendous hullabaloo outside his office, jumped out of his mini Jacuzzi and, wearing only a white fluffy dressing gown, stormed past the crowd, turned right at the Office for Traffic Jam Control, past the Department for Dog Dropping Removal and straight into Mr Smee's office.

"What in the name of King Ebenezer have you done this time?" shouted the Mayor in an almighty rage, waving his copy of the *Packet* in Mr Smee's face. "What did you think you were doing calling me a fibber? And how dare you tell him about my Jacuzzi and portable bar? The whole town will think I'm nothing but a loud-mouth liar with a taste for bubble bath and Brandy Highballs!" The Mayor's moustache bristled straight out as if he had been plugged into an electrical socket. "And what are all these people doing here?" he added, looking around him. "Is it pension day or something?"

"Er, the problem seems to have struck again, sir," said Mr Smee sheepishly.

"Oh for crying out loud!" exclaimed the Mayor. "Why don't you call the Chief of Police, then? I am sick and tired of being lumbered with this. It's about time he did his job."

"You *are* the Chief of Police," said Mr Smee quietly.

"And the School Governor and Head of the Lodge of Freewheeling Elks," added Mrs Britt-Dullforce.

"Damn," said the Mayor, annoyed at forgetting all his other jobs.

"And anyway," added Mr Smee, "someone appears to have chewed through the phone lines – so no one can call anyone at all."

"So who's the culprit?" demanded the Mayor.

Mr Smee looked at his long list of complaints and frowned. "Well I can safely say we're looking for someone who is either as small as a cat or over seven feet tall, wearing a crash helmet and a green belt with buttons, with long claws made of metal, with either springs or roller skates on his feet, who can jump as high as a house in one leap, who is either bald or has long shaggy hair and possibly feathers and who resembles an alien."

The Mayor's face turned the exact colour of a beetroot. "Smee, are you trying to make a fool out of me?" he bellowed.

"Absolutely 100 per cent not, sir," said Mr Smee.

"Right. Well I suggest you get to the bottom of this, and fast – or I shall demote you to the Department for Painting Lines in the Middle of the Road," barked the Mayor irritably. "And get the phone lines unchewed as well. I'm throwing an enormous and elaborate cocktail party tonight and I need to double my order of cocktail cherries."

And with that he stamped back out of the office huffily, pushing past the queue of complainers, past the Department for Dog Dropping Removal, left at the Office for Traffic Jam Control and back into his own office, where he climbed straight into his mini Jacuzzi in his dressing gown because in his anger he had forgotten to get undressed.

"He needs to get in touch with his inner calm," said Mrs Britt-Dullforce. "I'll bring in my aroma-therapy kit tomorrow and give him an emergency lavender treatment."

Aunt Nehemiah's Bunions

Mr Smee was racking his brains and trying to eat kidney stew at the same time. Which was not something he was used to having to do.

"It could be anyone or anything," he said, pointing a piece of offal at Solomon and waving it demonstratively. "It could be the Nutmeg Gang. Or aliens. For all we know it could be a pile of monkeys."

"Don't be stupid," snapped Aunt Nehemiah. "Monkeys are far too lazy and disorganized to do anything like this. No, it's those unruly youths that Mr Chatterjee is always being far too nice to. No discipline at school these days, that's the problem. Why, in my day if you spoke out of turn you'd get six of the best with an extra large plimsoll and then be locked in the store cupboard for a week with just rats for company."

But Solomon was not sure that Mr Smee was so far from the truth. Monkeys, thought Solomon quietly to himself. It was possible, he supposed. But where were they now? And if they were still here, what would they get up to next? But his thoughts were interrupted by Aunt Nehemiah.

"Stop daydreaming at once. In my day there were no daydreams. We were lucky even to dream at night, what with having to get up every hour to chop logs for the fire lest we froze to our sheets. Now eat that kidney up and then you can brush the raven feathers on my best hat."

"Why?" asked Solomon. "Are you going to Mayor Plusfour's enormous and elaborate cocktail party tonight?"

"No I am not," snapped Aunt Nehemiah. "I do not believe in parties. They are dangerous places, full of sinful dancing and merriment. Nor do I believe in cocktails, which are a waste of paper umbrellas. In my day we didn't have cocktails. We were lucky to drink ditch water out of a tin bucket."

Solomon had an idea and turned to Mr Smee.

"What about you, Dad? Are you going to the party? You might see Lysandra there."

"Don't be daft," said Mr Smee, and laughed. "The Mayor hasn't invited me. And anyway, I don't expect Lysandra would even remember who I am. It's been twenty-six years, you know!"

"I don't know what you would want to see that girl for anyway," snapped Aunt Nehemiah. "She was a spoilt child who never had to do a day's work in her life, and now she's grown up she'll be even worse."

Mr Smee sighed. "Well I do have other things to think about. Like the menace."

"Well you'd better hurry up or it'll be long gone," said Aunt Nehemiah. "You slowcoaches couldn't catch a sloth with sleeping sickness."

Solomon rolled his eyes. His father smiled at him.

"Now I'm off to soak my bunions in onion water and I do not want disturbing." And Aunt Nehemiah stalked off to the bathroom and shut the door.

But the menace was not long gone at all. It was actually closer than any of them could have imagined. In fact, at that very moment it was creeping past the window and up the fire escape, heading straight for Aunt Nehemiah's bedroom.

The Poo in the Shoe

An hour later, Solomon and Mr Smee were still downstairs trying to work out what could have caused the various chaotic events of the past few days when Aunt Nehemiah bellowed down from the top of the stairs.

"Solomon Smee, get up here immediately!"

"What have you done now, Solomon?" asked Mr Smee.

"Oh cripes!" said Solomon. "Her hat. I forgot to brush the feathers on her hat."

And he ran upstairs, followed by Mr Smee ready to placate Aunt Nehemiah in case things got messy.

But when they arrived things were already messy. Very messy indeed.

Aunt Nehemiah towered in the doorway, her feet smelling of onions, her hairy wart pulsating and her eyes flashing like a demon's. Behind her was a scene of utter devastation. All Aunt Nehemiah's clothes had been flung out of the wardrobe onto the floor, which was now a sea of grey sackcloth, reinforced girdles and scary big black pants. The lock on her medicine cabinet appeared to have been chewed off, and several creams and ointments were now open and oozing out all over the table. Her hat-boxes, of which there were several, were no longer stacked on top of the wardrobe but were crushed and empty on the floor. All that remained of their contents was a single raven feather, which floated slowly down to the floor in front of Solomon.

"Crikey," he said.

"What have you been up to in here, you horrible child? Where are my hats and why is there wart remover all over the portrait of Great-Uncle Boanerges?" shouted Aunt Nehemiah. Solomon peered at the painting. It was ruined. The formerly stiff and fearsome man looked like a clown with white creamy hair and a big fluffy beard to match.

"I don't know, Aunt," said Solomon. "It wasn't me. I've been downstairs with Dad, working on the mystery."

"Don't give me that!" shouted Aunt Nehemiah.

"I know what you small boys get up to with your cheating and lying and a hundred other kinds of evil."

"But it's true," said Mr Smee. "We've been downstairs the whole time."

Aunt Nehemiah hurrumphed. "Well if it's not you then it must be those unruly boys escaped from their institution. I am going to see Mr Chatterjee right now and give him a piece of my mind. Those boys want locking up in a room with big gnashing metal rabbit traps on all the doors in case they try to get out."

"But why would they steal your hats?" asked Solomon.

"They must be dressing up to disguise themselves," snapped Aunt Nehemiah. "Now, where are my shoes? Aha!" And she poked her bony oniony feet into her nun's black lace-ups.

"That's odd," said Aunt Nehemiah. "One of them feels warm." Solomon looked at her feet and his eyes widened in shock. Squeezing over the side of one shoe and all over Aunt Nehemiah's foot was something wet and brown and revolting. There was no mistaking what it was.

"A poo!" she cried. "There's a poo in my shoe!" She screamed and flung the shoe off, which only made matters worse because her foot was covered in the brown sticky stuff and she started treading it into the long woolly bits of the rug. The smell was horrible.

"Call Barry Chatterjee, now!" shrieked Aunt Nehemiah, waving her foot at Mr Smee. "Get him here immediately!" But Mr Smee backed up against the wall trying to keep away from the poo.

Solomon thought to himself. It couldn't have been Mr Chatterjee's boys. They were tied up with parcel string – Mr Ganges had said so. And anyway, awful though they were, they would never, ever do a poo in a shoe.

But who – or what – else could it be? They had to be small enough to get in all the tiny windows.

He ruled out elves, leprechauns, gnomes and other small mythical beings.

It could be contortionists or India-rubber men, but why all the fruit going missing? They got well paid for their acts. No, it had to be an animal.

And if it was an animal... Well it couldn't be elephants, zebras, dogs or tigers – they didn't have the fingers to get up to the mechanical mischief at Mr Ganges' garage.

They had to be able to climb up very high, but it couldn't be birds – it was the wrong sort of poo.

Then he remembered what his dad had said last night. It made sense. Small, hairy, nimble, with a liking for bananas and custard.

"Monkeys," he said. "It's definitely monkeys."

"Not monkeys, you idiot boy, it's marauding children," cried Aunt Nehemiah, hopping around with her brown smelly foot in front of her.

"No, Dad, it really is monkeys. Think about it. The bananas going missing, the 'hooping' noise that people have been hearing. Monkeys have sharp claws as well – I know they're not made of metal, but I think Mr Jambutty may have made that up."

"Are you sure, Solomon?" asked Mr Smee. "Are you 110 per cent absolutely no doubt about it sure?"

"There's no such thing as 110 per cent," said Aunt Nehemiah.

But Solomon ignored her. "I'm sure."

"Very well," said Mr Smee, "then I shall tell Mayor Plusfour first thing in the morning." And he gave Solomon a hug.

But the Mayor was about to find out for himself.

The Enormous and Elaborate Cocktail Party

At the same time, on the right side of Royal Nerdal Norton, the Mayor was hosting his enormous and elaborate cocktail party.

There was nothing the Mayor liked better than to show off at a good party. Last year he had installed a marble sperm whale in the garden that spouted pink champagne from its blow-hole. This year he had gone for a jungle theme. The house had been decorated from top to bottom with coconut trees by the Mayor's much put-upon servant Minoo. There were pineapple-flavoured cocktails all round, and to top it off the Mayor had ordered a band of acrobats called the "Krankee Krowd" to dress as jungle animals and entertain his guests.

It was truly magnificent and all of Royal Nerdal Norton was there to see it.

Mr Ganges and Mr Jambutty were there in their

best Sunday suits.

Mrs Perambulator was there in a new peach georgette bat-wing gown from the Fancypants Frock Parlour on Malabar Street.

Mr Bottleopener was there too, along with Mrs Samovar, Manjit the postman and several army majors in full dress uniform.

But (apart from Mr Smee, Aunt Nehemiah and Solomon) there was one person who was not there. The Mayor's beautiful daughter, Lysandra.

Lysandra never went to the Mayor's parties because she was not invited. The Mayor did not want any of the other guests getting ideas about her and trying to woo her away from him. But Lysandra didn't mind too much. She wasn't one for razzle-dazzle and glitz. She thought it was just showing off. Instead she preferred to sit upstairs in the library in her jeans and T-shirt and read the newspapers. But tonight she rather wanted to catch a glimpse of the acrobats. Lysandra had always dreamt of running away with a circus, seeing faraway places and doing death-defying stunts and being somewhere the Mayor was not. Once upon a time she and her friends had practised headstands and cartwheels in the garden in case a circus ever came to town. But those days were distant memories now.

So she decided that after she had finished reading Boyce Spink's latest article she would sneak down to the main staircase and watch between the banisters.

"Council in Catastrophe Cover-up!" proclaimed the headline.

What a load of twaddle, thought Lysandra to herself. Aliens indeed. Everyone knows aliens don't exist.

But one name caught her eye. A name from long ago. "Mild-mannered Complaints Officer Harry Smee," she read. Then it went on, "Tragic single father Mr Haroon Smee, 34..."

"But it can't be, can it?" she said to herself. "It would make him exactly the right age. But a single father – oh poor, poor Harry."

But before she could find out any more about her old friend Harry she heard the doorbell ring, playing a high, tinny version of "Hark the Herald Angels Sing".

That will be them, thought Lysandra excitedly. She folded the paper for later, crept quietly out of the library in her slippers and settled herself on the landing.

Through the banisters she saw Minoo, dressed

in smart livery with a grass skirt over the top as a concession to the jungle theme, run to answer the door.

"Good evening," said Minoo.

On the doorstep were sixty-seven small, hairy fellows, several wearing black feathered hats. "Ah, you must be the 'Krankee Krowd'," said Minoo. "I am most pleased to greet you to the home of our honourable Mayor." And he ushered them in.

The Mayor was standing in the hallway chatting loudly to Mrs Perambulator about the time he had single-handedly wrestled an alligator to death, when he saw the new arrivals. "Oh, the Krankees! Superb costumes, chaps," said the Mayor. "Right on the button. I like the headdresses – most tribal. Now feel free to help yourselves to a cocktail and some nibbles and then as soon as you're ready let's see what you can do!"

"You'll love these men," he said to Mrs Perambulator, twiddling his waxed moustache and leering revoltingly at her. "They do a special trick where they all form a pyramid and the top one balances on his head while juggling plates with his feet and simultaneously playing a kazoo."

"Oooh, Horace!" giggled Mrs Perambulator.

"Rather quiet, aren't they?" said Mr Ganges as the troupe wandered around among the guests.

"Maybe they're from one of those mute fig-eating tribes," said Mr Jambutty. "I hear they make terribly good trapeze acts – low centre of gravity, you know, and no complaining when they fall."

"Well they certainly are acrobatic," said Mr Bottle-opener to Mr Ganges, Mr Jambutty and Minoo. "Look up there." They looked. One of the troupe was swinging nimbly from a crystal chandelier.

"Oh, sir," said Minoo to the acrobat. "I do not think your act can involve the lighting. The Mayor is very particular about who touches his priceless artefacts."

The acrobat flung himself off, somersaulted onto the top of the banister and slid backwards down to the bottom.

"Bravo!" cheered the guests.

"Hoop!" shrieked the acrobat.

Lysandra, who had a splendid view from her vantage point at the top of the stairs, was just thinking that "hoop" was a very odd thing for an acrobat to say when the phone rang with a calypso version of "God Save the King". As the Mayor was busy feeding Mrs Perambulator glacé cherries out of the jar by poking them with a cocktail stick, Minoo answered it instead.

"Mmm, hmm. Mmm, hmm. I see." And he put the phone down and went to see the Mayor.

"That was the Krankees, sir," said Minoo. "Their bus has broken down on the bypass five miles out of town and one of their tumblers has wrenched his funny bone trying to change the wheel. They say they are terribly sorry but there's nothing they can do." Then he realized what he had said. As did the Mayor. A funny look came over his face. First he turned red, then white, then purple.

"But if the Krankees are on the bypass," he yelled, "then exactly who are in my cocktail lounge in monkey suits drinking pina coladas?"

"Furry criminals with tails?" suggested Minoo.

"Furry criminals? With tails?" shouted the Mayor. "Minoo, you pea-brained porter. Those aren't monkey costumes. Those are real monkeys."

"Oh deary me," said Minoo. "The banquet! Quick!"

The Mayor was right. It was not midgets, or aliens, or the Nutmeg Gang, or the Anti-Custard League, but

84

sixty-seven small brown monkeys. And right now they were peering around the cocktail lounge in delight. A vast feast was laid out on two trestle tables with a stack of paper plates and napkins, and the monkeys wasted no time in sampling the wares. Before anyone could stop them they had eaten hams and yams, small pastries like jewels, pomegranates and peacock eggs in aspic. They worked their way through two bowls of custard and tapioca and then stamped on a plate of cream cakes, which oozed nicely between their toes and made a fantastic mess. Then they threw grapes at each other, trying to catch them in their mouths (which they were not very good at) before inserting a plate of pigeon in a rose-petal sauce into the Mayor's brand-new video recorder, which was on display to show off to his guests.

At the door to the cocktail lounge the Mayor stopped dead in shock. His feast was ruined. Instead of the fine display of food and flowers was a scene of flying fur, displaced puddings and fruit and a good deal of squawking and hooping.

The Mayor did not know what to say. Which was quite unusual for the Mayor. (But then would *you* know what to say if sixty-seven monkeys had ransacked your house when guests had just turned up for cocktails?) So he did what he always did when something went wrong – he blamed it on someone else.

"Minoo, you twit, come here immediately. This is all your fault, you slow-witted servant. I demand that you—" But he was cut off by a monkey who swung past him on the curtain tassels and jumped onto his head.

"Horace, what is the meaning of these monkeys?" demanded Mrs Perambulator. "I do not think it is appropriate at all."

But the Mayor was still covered in monkey, and all he could say was "gggllmph".

"Come on, Mr Ganges," said Mr Jambutty. "I think we had best be off."

"Quite right, Mr Jambutty," said Mr Ganges.

They, and the rest of the guests, grabbed their coats and hats and fled out of the front door towards home.

Following behind them were a long line of monkeys and Minoo, who was trying to catch them with a butterfly net.

The Mayor was apoplectic with anger. "Aliens and

bandits?" he snorted after he had wrested himself clear of the monkey that had been clinging onto his moustache. "Just wait until I get my hands on Smee in the morning. He'll be demoted to the Department of Recovering Overdue Library Books faster than he can say jumping Jehosaphat!" And he went to have a large and elaborate cocktail to calm his nerves.

The only person who was happy about the evening's events was Lysandra, who sat on the grand staircase in her slippers. It was without doubt the most fun she had had in years. "Poor Dad," she laughed to herself. "He won't be having any more parties for a while." And she laughed again. "Monkeys. Millions of marvellous monkeys in hats. How funny!"

The Royal Emergency Wild Animal Corps

"Monkeys!" shouted the Mayor at Mr Smee when he got into the office the next morning. "Millions of horrible hairy little monkeys in hats."

"So Solomon was right!" said Mr Smee.

"I don't care what Solomon thinks of anything. And anyway, who's Solomon?" But he didn't wait to find out. "What I care about is my poor Lysandra, who has no doubt caught some unmentionable disease from them and may drop dead – and then you shall be to blame. Not to mention that my enormous and elaborate cocktail party was utterly ruined and like as not I shall be the laughing-stock of Royal Nerdal Norton. Now do something immediately or I will demote you to the Unit of Public Toilet Polishing."

"But what shall I do?" asked Mr Smee.

"Call the army, you buffoon! Get me the Royal

Emergency Wild Animal Corps and make sure they are armed with exceptionally long knives and clubs with pointy bits on them."

"But Mayor," protested Mrs Britt-Dullforce, "I think you'll find that in Subsection C, Paragraph 20 of the Simians in a Public Place Act (Amended), we are not allowed to chop up or otherwise damage monkeys. We have to trap them humanely, then send them to a sanctuary where they can eat fruit and express themselves in creative ways."

"What?" gurgled the Mayor. "Who passed this idiotic law?"

"Er, you did, sir," replied Mr Smee.

"Damn and bother," said the Mayor. "You and your Monkey Protection League!" he added, staring pointedly at Mrs Britt-Dullforce.

"So, what shall I tell the army?" asked Mr Smee.

"Tell them to bring big cages and inspiration. And call me when you're done!" he said angrily, stomping back to his office where he poured himself a large gin and cherryade from his portable lounge bar (even though it wasn't even lunchtime).

"Monkeys," said Solomon proudly from the wastepaper bin. "I knew it." But knowing it was not as easy as fixing it. And this monkey menace was going to take some very big fixing indeed.

The Royal Emergency Wild Animal Corps was a small and rather ill-trained unit, as there was not much call for wild-animal trapping in Royal Nerdal Norton. The last time they had had an emergency was when Mr Ganges found an unusually large beetle in his downstairs lavatory. They were led by Colonel Snell, who was an enthusiastic – if not entirely competent – man who had been trans-ferred from the Royal Emergency Knotmaking Regiment after a fatal incident involving a brigadier and some baling twine.

"We have managed to locate the troublesome little blighters," said Colonel Snell, waving a pair of binoculars at Mr Smee. "They are at this very moment assembled at the Arthur Gomez Memorial Bandstand making a most tremendous racket with the instruments. The band members them-selves have had to evacuate the area and are now being dosed with headache pills by the St Derek's Ambulance Brigade."

"Good, good," said Mr Smee. "And how exactly

do you intend to catch the monkeys?"

"Fishing-rods and French fancies," said Colonel Snell. "It's an ancient method which is almost 99 per cent successful."

"How does it work?" asked Solomon, who had come along to watch.

"Very simple. We attach the delicious French fancies to the fishing-lines and cover them in extra-strong glue, then we dangle them in front of the monkeys to tempt them. Then when they bite, we reel them in quick!"

"Very well," said Mr Smee, not quite convinced. "Let's go." And off marched Mr Smee, Solomon, Colonel Snell, the rest of the Royal Emergency Wild Animal Corps and several hangers-on, to the bandstand where the monkeys were making an unholy din with a bassoon, a trumpet and the entire percussion section. The band members who had fought to the last to save their instruments were now sitting in a bedraggled group on the grass, being interviewed by Boyce Spink.

"Are you sure this is going to work, Dad?" whispered Solomon. "I don't think the monkeys are going to fall for this."

"Well we have to hope – because if it doesn't work then I will be moved to the Unit of Public Toilet Polishing and you will be back at home with Aunt Nehemiah for the rest of the holidays," replied Mr Smee.

Solomon gulped, deciding to keep his mouth shut and his fingers crossed.

"Right, men," ordered Colonel Snell in a loud army manner. "French fancies at the ready!" The soldiers pulled out a large pot of glue and a box of pink and yellow iced cakes.

"Men, arm your rods!" ordered Colonel Snell. Using a large brush the soldiers painted glue all over the fancies, managing to get a lot of it on themselves and on the crowd of bystanders that was growing by the minute.

"Ready!" said Colonel Snell. The crowd ooh-ed and ahh-ed loudly.

"Aim!" The crowd held its breath.

"Fire!" he shouted, and the soldiers cast their pink and yellow cakes towards the bandstand.

The monkeys had been watching this intently, because although they had enjoyed making a noise with the instruments, they liked cake with icing on it a good deal more. When the French fancies flew their way they all hooped excitedly and jumped in the air to catch them. But unfortunately Colonel Snell had got his metres muddled up with his inches and measured the fishing-lines all wrong. The fancies sailed right over the monkeys' heads and into the crowd on the other side of the bandstand, showering everyone with sponge cake and icing, and glueing Maureen and Doreen Perambulator together. Mr Smee and Solomon sighed.

"That's what will happen if you try to restrict God's own creatures," said Mrs Britt-Dullforce as she, Mr Smee and Solomon walked back to the office, leaving the chaos behind them. But Mr Smee was not listening. He was worrying about what the Mayor would say. And he was right to.

"Call the Department for Park and Bandstand Sweeping immediately, to clean up the mess," said the Mayor when Mr Smee telephoned him to explain the lack of captured monkeys and the abundance of people with glue and French-fancy trimmed outfits queuing outside his office. "And transfer Colonel Snell to the Gardening Battalion, where he can't cause any more damage."

"Yes, sir," said Mr Smee. "But what shall I do about the monkeys?"

"First thing in the morning you must call Maurice Hankey."

"Maurice Hankey the Court Magician? Are you sure?"

"Don't you dare question me, you, you ... clerk!" barked the Mayor. "Just call up Hankey, and if that doesn't work you can start packing your belongings into a box to take round to the Office of Pigeon Feeding Licence Application." And he slammed the phone down just to make double sure Mr Smee knew he meant business.

Mr Smee sighed again. "Not Maurice Hankey," he said, and he let his head drop on the desk in despair. "Ow," he added.

Maurice Hankey the Court Magician

While Mr Smee was none too pleased about the idea, Maurice Hankey was delighted to be given something official to do. He had been rather short of work at the palace since he had accidentally turned the Queen's favourite pony, Rex, into a chocolate selection box. To fill the time he had been working part-time at Mr Bottleopener's chemist shop, where he had caused some bother by making up prescriptions of his own. Several customers had complained of sprouting extra fingers or burping green sulphurous bubbles at inappropriate moments.

He turned up the next morning at 9 a.m. sharp with a large velvet bag full of coloured handkerchiefs, a tall green wizard's hat with purple stars on it, a silvery cloak and a wand.

Overnight, the monkeys had taken up residence

in the gardens of the General Hospital, and a large crowd, including Boyce Spink and his tape recorder, had already gathered among the azaleas to see the latest plan to get rid of the pests.

"Got any comment for the *Packet*?" asked Boyce Spink.

"Yes – go away," said the Mayor.

Boyce flicked the switch on his recorder. "The tension is clearly getting to the Mayor, who of course stands to lose his high-powered job if the menace is not put behind bars by the end of the week."

"Oh put a sock in it, Spink," said the Mayor.

Boyce Spink slid the recorder back into his macintosh pocket and smiled sneakily.

"Right, everyone, stand well back," said Maurice Hankey, waving his wand around in a worrying manner – spells had been known in the past to fly out by accident. "Today's magic will be particularly potent and I cannot be held responsible for any accidents."

The crowd tutted. Maurice always claimed he couldn't be held responsible for accidents, even when he had turned his own mother into a large beef casserole.

"What are you going to do to the monkeys?" Mr Smee asked.

"First of all I am going to cast a special calming spell to stop them moving about so much," said Maurice importantly. "Then I am going to use an ancient incantation to make them decide to take a long touring holiday to the Congo. And if that fails I'll turn them all into cockroaches and stamp on them."

Mr Smee crossed his fingers for luck. He was going to need plenty of it. Solomon did the same.

"Right, on your marks ... get set ... alakazam!" shouted Maurice. A line of sparkly electricity shot out of the end of his wand and missed the monkeys completely. Instead it hit Mrs Perambulator and sent her into a deep and very snorey sleep.

The crowd clapped. All except the Mayor, who was jumping up and down with anger – not easy to do when you're as big as the Mayor.

"Hankey!" he shouted at Maurice.

Maurice waved his wand again quickly and conjured up a large knickerbocker glory with cherry sauce, which he gave to the Mayor to calm him down. Which it did.

Mr Smee shook his head.

Then Maurice tried again. This time a purple flame shot out of the end of the wand, exploded and showered the crowd with strawberry bonbons. "Hurrah!" they all shouted, although it sounded more like "Hgggh huugh!" because their mouths were all stuck together with chewy toffee. "Hoop!" squawked the monkeys, who could still talk even with toffees in their mouths, which is one of their secrets.

"Oh catastrophic cats!" said Maurice, more than a little put out by his own failure. He jabbed his wand in the air, sending out a trail of sparks, singeing a small monkey and turning Doreen Perambulator's ears blue.

"Maurice, you moron," said the Mayor, who had just finished his knickerbocker glory and was annoyed again.

"Don't moan at me, Mayor," said Maurice. "I didn't bring the monkeys here. I could just as well be at home reading my caravanning magazines."

The crowd, on the other hand, was enjoying every minute of it.

"Oh, most impressive," laughed Mr Jambutty.

"Think it's funny, do you, Jambutty?" demanded

100

Maurice in a squeaky voice, and he zapped him with a spell that covered him from head to foot in cold porridge.

But Solomon wasn't watching this. He was looking around, shaking his head.

"Dad, where have the monkeys gone?"

Mr Smee looked around. The monkeys had vanished.

"It can't have been Maurice," he said. "He hasn't done a single successful spell all day."

"I think they got bored," said Solomon.

He was right. In all the kerfuffle the monkeys had slunk off to look for something else to play with.

"Sir," said Mr Smee, leaning over towards the Mayor. "Sir, don't be upset, but I think the monkeys have run away."

"What?" demanded the Mayor. He looked around. The hospital grounds were full of people with odd-coloured ears and noses, singed eyebrows and mouths full of toffee. But there was not a single monkey to be seen.

"Oops," said Maurice.

"Oops?" said the Mayor. "OOPS?! I'll give you oops! I'm banning any magic except at Christmas and on bank holidays. And as for you, Smee, tidy up this mess immediately or you'll spend the rest of your days as the most junior clerk in the Office of Sewage Inspection."

"But what about the monkeys, sir?" asked Mr Smee.

"I don't know. I need a drink to think," said the Mayor.

"Mayor says 'I haven't got a clue'," said Boyce Spink, who had fished his recorder back out of his pocket and was frantically dictating notes for tomorrow's front page.

"Right, that does it," said the Mayor, and he grabbed Boyce Spink's tape recorder and stamped on it. Then he picked up the remains and threw them in the fountain, before stomping off to leave Mr Smee to deal with Maurice, the monkeys, Boyce Spink and Mrs Perambulator, who was still asleep on a bed of snapdragons.

"Now what?" wondered Solomon to himself.

More Monkeys

"Bigger monkeys," said the Mayor triumphantly to Mr Smee the next day. "That'll scare the smaller monkeys into submission. Langurs, big fearsome ones with gnashing teeth, filthy fur and filthier tempers."

The Mayor had a large cocktail in his hand and was back to his normal loud and full of bad ideas self after yesterday's mayhem.

"But Mayor," said Mrs Britt-Dullforce, "langurs are terribly tricky to persuade to do anything at the best of times. And anyway, we can't force them to do any jobs they don't want to – it's in Paragraph 4, line 133 of the Employment of Apes Act."

"Then hire them as civil servants and pay them 600 rupees a month," barked the Mayor, determined not to let one of his good ideas go to waste.

Solomon, who was back in his wastepaper bin,

was not too sure about this at all. He pulled his pen out of his shirt pocket, picked up a piece of waste paper and scribbled a note, which he pushed out of the lid towards his dad.

Mr Smee tried not to look shocked and glanced down at it.

"Er. But sir, they haven't got any pockets to keep money in. And, er, even if they did, what would they spend it on?" he said, reading Solomon's note.

"We'll just pay them in bananas, then," said the Mayor, as if this was obvious – which it was not. And he took a slurp of his cocktail before posting the glass into the wastepaper bin.

"Ugggh," said the bin.

"What was that?"

"Nothing, sir," said Mr Smee. "Mrs Britt-Dullforce has a little wind."

"Not again," said the Mayor, and stomped off to pour himself another cocktail.

Before Mrs Britt-Dullforce could kick up a stink about the wind that she didn't have, Mr Smee grabbed a sticky Solomon out of the bin and flew out of the door.

"Where are we going, Dad?" asked Solomon.

"To get bigger monkeys," said Mr Smee.

"But Dad, you know it won't work," protested Solomon.

Mr Smee stopped and crouched down in front of his son. "Solomon my boy, I know it's preposterous, but what can I do? I have to do what the Mayor tells me."

"Even if it's wrong?" asked Solomon.

"I'm afraid so," said his dad.

Solomon sighed and nodded. Mr Smee took his hand.

"Now come on, we've got work to do."

So the two of them set off to the Fur and Feathers Amazing Animal Emporium, where they hired ten enormous langurs. As Solomon had predicted, trouble was not long in coming.

First of all the langurs refused to get on board the bus into town until Mr Smee gave them an extra banana apiece. And then they spent the whole journey picking fleas out of each other's filthy armpits and hanging from the luggage racks. The bus driver was not happy.

"Mr Smee, this is not on," he said. "Not only have their smaller cousins wrecked my Royal Nerdal

Norton Express, into which I had only just installed an iced tea, coffee and Bovril dispenser, but now I am going to have to spend a day hosing this out to get rid of the insects and smell." So Mr Smee had to pay him extra. Things were not going well.

As soon as they arrived at their destination – the Limpopo and Limpopo department store – they discovered the smaller monkeys causing havoc in the shoe section, where Mr Jambutty, Mr Ganges and the Perambulators had been trying to buy sandals, work boots and three pairs of pink stilettos respectively.

"Oh thank goodness you are here, Mr Smee," said Mr Limpopo senior. "It is an utter and absolute world-class disaster all round. The monkeys have eaten three dozen pairs of plimsolls and taken the laces out of all the gentlemen's brogues, which they are now using as an enormous lasso."

"They have already hoop-la'd Mrs Perambulator," added Mr Limpopo junior, wringing his hands.

But they were not quite so happy to see Mr Smee and Solomon when they saw what they had brought with him.

"Lord above!" said Mr Limpopo senior. "What are these unsanitary and oversized creatures doing here? They will surely contaminate my entire stock with their infestations."

"Yes, my thoughts exactly," added Mr Limpopo junior, who did not like to let his father have the last word on anything.

"Er, do not fret," said Mr Smee, trying to sound in charge. "These are a highly trained gang – and what's more, they are in my full employ, so I will remain in control at all times." But he did not even believe himself.

Meanwhile the langurs were eyeing the smaller monkeys with interest. The smaller monkeys eyed the langurs right back. Then it started. A small monkey picked up a black patent-leather winkle-picker and hurled it right at the biggest big monkey.

The big monkey let out a bloodcurdling shriek and leapt over a bargain bucket of plastic sandals towards the smaller monkeys, followed by the rest of the angry and stinking langurs. The smaller monkeys hooped at the tops of their voices and started chucking wellingtons at them. The langurs retaliated by grabbing some extremely pointy steel-toecapped boots and throwing them into the fray.

Then one of the smaller monkeys let out a long,

low call and headed towards the escalators with his sixty-six friends behind him. The langurs set off in hot pursuit, followed by Mr Limpopo senior, Mr Limpopo junior, Mr Smee, Solomon, Mr Jambutty, Mr Ganges and the Perambulators.

The monkeys loved the moving metal staircase and hooped with delight as they rode upwards. At the top was the tableware section. "Oh my blessed stars, not the prize porcelain!" cried Mr Limpopo senior.

Mr Limpopo junior went to add something, but too late... A tremendous crashing and tinkling sound came from the first floor.

The crowd arrived at the top of the staircase to what looked like the world's most unsuccessful crockery-juggling monkeys act. A succession of plates, serving bowls, cappuccino mugs, sugar bowls and saucers came whizzing through the air and smashed into a thousand smithereens on the lino floor.

"I knew we should have invested in shag-pile carpet," said Mr Limpopo junior bitterly as he cowered behind a cash desk.

"I blame the government," added Mr Jambutty, who thought the government was to blame for everything, even the weather.

Meanwhile, Solomon, who had been watching the commotion intently, noticed something odd. "Dad, look at the monkeys," he said.

Mr Smee looked around. The monkeys had stopped fighting and seemed to be grooming each other.

"Oh dear, I don't like the look of this," said Mr Smee.

"It's not good, is it, Dad?" said Solomon.

"No," said Mr Smee, "not good at all."

He was right. The monkeys together were a formidable force. And they knew it. They shrieked and jumped back on the down escalator and rode towards the ground floor.

"Quick, after them!" said Mr Limpopo senior.

"Yes, double quick!" said Mr Limpopo junior.

Falling over each other in the rush the crowd headed to the escalator only to find they had to walk down because it had been jammed by a monkey pressing the red emergency button on and off too many times at the bottom.

Downstairs a most worrying turn of events was taking place. The monkeys had found the kitchenware section and were brandishing forks, mashers, meat skewers and electric whisks.

"Arm yourselves, quick!" shouted Mr Limpopo senior. Solomon grabbed a filleting knife, Mr Smee found a steak mallet and Maureen and Doreen picked up a fizzy drink maker, which they thought they could keep as a souvenir if it didn't work as a weapon.

The langurs snarled and whirred their electric egg-scramblers. The smaller monkeys hooped and banged their forks around. Mr Ganges feebly waved a potato peeler.

But before an almighty fight could break out a large bellow came from the direction of the jumbo pants departments.

"Mr Smee, stop this at once." The voice was so loud and important that the monkeys stopped hooping in shock, and everyone dropped their kitchenware with a clatter. Standing in front of a selection of extra-large, reinforced gusset Y-fronts, with her hands on her hips and a face like thunder, was Mrs Britt-Dullforce.

"Oh hellfire!" said Solomon.

"Language!" said Mr Smee.

"Mr Smee!" shouted his secretary. "This has gone

112

too far. You are contravening several employment laws and most of the Monkey Welfare Acts besides. I am here to lead the langurs on a strike. There will be no more work until they get equal pay and better conditions, including three weeks' paid holiday and more frequent biscuit breaks."

"Oh shut up," said Mr Limpopo senior. "How can they strike when they're not working in the first place."

"Yes!" said Mr Limpopo junior.

Mrs Britt-Dullforce thought for a moment. "Hmm. Well this is clearly their own way of expressing industrial action; the whisks and mashers are symbols of oppression by mankind. Now get out of my way."

Mr Limpopo senior did as he was told. There was clearly no arguing with Mrs Britt-Dullforce.

"Monkeys run free!" she shouted as she flung the doors open wide. "Eat bananas, scamper playfully!"

The monkeys seized their chance and ran off into town.

Mr Smee sat down on the floor with his head in his hands. "Doomed," he said. "I am completely and most intolerably doomed."

Solomon Has Some Ideas

M r Smee was still worrying about the monkeys at teatime.

"But Dad, you always tell me there's an answer to everything," said Solomon.

"No there isn't!" snapped Aunt Nehemiah as they sat down to boiled brains for tea. "What about 'What comes at the end of the universe?' Hah, that's stumped you, hasn't it? Or 'Why does no one ever see baby pigeons?'"

Solomon looked at her hairy wart quivering under her nose and seethed inwardly. Outward seething in front of Aunt Nehemiah was not to be advised.

"Your aunt is right, Solomon," said Mr Smee sadly. "Maybe this is one of those things that we'll never know how to solve."

But Solomon was not so sure. There had to be a way to catch the monkeys. That night, as he lay on his little wooden bed with the yellow candlewick cover, in the small house on the wrong side of Royal Nerdal Norton, he thought and thought. Then he had an idea. He reached up to the top shelf above his bed and pulled down the "M" volume of his encyclopaedia. On the red leather spine it had gold embossed letters, which read: "Macadamia to Myxomatosis".

Under **Monkey** it said: "*n.* Any of a large and various group of mammals of the order of primates. Excellent climbers, and primarily arboreal."

Solomon looked up "arboreal" and found it meant they lived in trees. Then he went back to the monkey definition.

"Nearly all live in tropical or subtropical climates. Their eyes point forward and their hands and feet are highly developed for grasping. Monkeys live in troops of up to one hundred individuals and often travel about in search of food and fun."

Very interesting, thought Solomon, but not very helpful. So he picked up his *Children's Colour Dictionary.*

In that he learnt that "monkey nut" was another word for "peanut", that there was a tree called a "monkey puzzle" and that a "monkey's wedding" was not anything to do with marriage but a strange weather condition where it was rainy and sunny all at the same time.

He looked in old comic books for ideas, but in there all the superheroes had special weapons, like invisibility buttons or jet boots.

Solomon thought and thought but couldn't find an answer, until slowly, his mind full of monkeys, he drifted off to sleep.

But on the right side of town, in a big pink house with pillars and chandeliers and a swirly carpet, someone else was thinking about the monkeys too. In the Mayor's library Lysandra was reading old newspaper reports. Every day, when an article caught her fancy she filed it safely away in a big black leather box. It was her way of keeping in touch with the outside world that she had not seen for so many years.

"Oh, Harry," she said sorrowfully as she read another story of his misfortune with the monkeys. "I wish I were there to help you. But I don't know what the answer is, I really don't." And she clipped out the story neatly and dropped it into the big leather box. Then she shut the lid, put the scissors safely away in a drawer, switched out the library light and trod slowly down the landing to bed.

Mr Smee's Bright Idea

By the next morning the situation had got completely out of control. Led by the enormous langurs the monkeys had taken over two floors of the Municipal Offices. What's more, an enormous crowd had gathered outside Mr Smee's office to protest about the situation.

"I am declaring a state of Municipal emergency," shouted the Mayor, bursting into Mr Smee's office before Solomon had even had a chance to get into the bin. "The monkeys are stealing state secrets and tampering with the phone hotlines. They have even raided my lounge bar: several of them are now enjoying a martini in the comfort of my mini Jacuzzi, where I am not at all sure they are obeying the rules about not weeing in the water."

Then he caught sight of Solomon. "And what on earth is that? Some kind of hideous hairless monkey?"

"Er no, sir, it's my son Solomon."

"What's he doing here?"

"Umm. Well, you see..." Mr Smee racked his brains. He had to think – and fast. If failing to catch monkeys wasn't a sackable offence then hiding his son in a wastepaper bin definitely was. But wait – he had it!

"He has an idea. Yes, that's it. An idea to catch the monkeys," said Mr Smee, and he sighed with relief.

"Are you sure?" demanded the Mayor.

"Yes, Dad, are you sure?" said Solomon, his eyes wide with fear. As you and I both know he had thought for hours the previous night and not come up with a single thing.

"What sort of idea?" said the Mayor.

Mr Smee thought. And thought. And thought.

"An amazing automatic monkey-catching machine," he said finally.

"A what?" said the Mayor.

"A what?" said Solomon.

"An amazing automatic monkey-catching machine," said Mr Smee.

Solomon fidgeted nervously. "Er, that's right," he said. "It will be a fantastical machine that will catch the monkeys and save the day for everyone," said Solomon, desperately wanting the Mayor to believe his dad.

"Oh really?" said the Mayor. "And where exactly is this wondrous invention?"

"Ah well, it's just in the blueprint stage," said Mr Smee. "A top inventor is working on it right now. But we'll have it for you by this afternoon, I promise."

"Yes, well make sure you do," said the Mayor, pulling his moustache. "Or it's off to the Department for Wasp Extermination for you. And as for you –" he bent over to look Solomon in the eye, and was so close that his moustache tickled Solomon's nose "– if this doesn't work then I'm sure there's a place for you in Barry Chatterjee's Home for Unruly Youth."

Solomon thought that Barry Chatterjee would be a picnic compared to being on his own with Aunt Nehemiah, but he didn't want to say so.

"Do you understand, boy?" said the Mayor.

Solomon nodded.

"Well, good," said the Mayor. And he stamped off down the corridor to shout at the monkeys in his Jacuzzi.

"Cripes!" said Solomon.

"What have we done?" wailed Mr Smee. "We're for it now!"

"No, Dad, we just need an inventor," said Solomon. "We'll be fine."

"But where will I find one?" said Mr Smee.

"In the phone book under 'I'?" suggested Solomon.

Mr Smee pulled down the fat yellow book and turned to the "I" section. "Icing experts," he read. "Inky stain removers... Ah, here it is. Inventors."

Solomon looked. Underneath was one small advert. "Terry Bunce – Inventor Extraordinaire," read Solomon aloud. "Ever heard of the 'self-tying shoe-lace' or the 'automatic pancake-flipper'?"

"No," said Mr Smee.

Solomon ignored him and read on. "Well they're all thanks to one man – Terry Bunce. Call Nerdal Norton 4434 today for a quote."

"He's our man," said Solomon. "He has to be. Call him now, Dad."

"OK," said Mr Smee. "Here goes." And he dialled carefully.

"Hello? Mr Bunce?" he said. "I wonder if you can help me."

124

Solomon hopped around him, trying to hear.

"Yes, I see. Mm-hmm. OK. Very well." And he put the phone down.

"What did he say, what did he say?" cried Solomon.

"Calm down, Solomon. Now he said he's not got time to do anything new but he does have an old invention that he might be able to adapt."

"Hurray!" shouted Solomon.

"Hmm. We'll see," said Mr Smee.

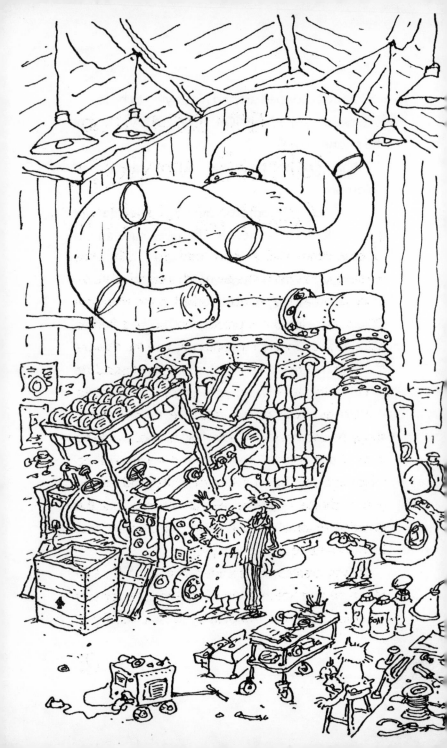

The Amazing Automatic Monkey-Catching Machine

Terry Bunce was a short, odd man with white whiskers who lived on his own with a cat called Kevin. Once upon a time he had worked in the Municipal Offices as a Tea-Urn Operator, but he had had to retire early on medical grounds because the Mayor's shouting had made him deaf in one ear. Instead he invented things, with varying degrees of success. Among his creations was a device to order your shopping and then work out what the price would be in thirty-two different countries, and a thingamabob which told you the time, brewed coffee and offered you a choice of newspaper all at once. But the Amazing Automatic Monkey-Catching Machine was his most ambitious invention yet.

"It was created for escaped chickens," he told Mr Smee and Solomon in a high-up-inventor sort of voice. "But I've adapted it to suit monkeys.

Would you like to see?"

They nodded.

"Very well," said Mr Bunce. "Come with me."

Solomon and Mr Smee followed Mr Bunce out the back of the house and down to an enormous shed at the bottom of the garden. Mr Bunce creaked open the enormous doors on their rusty hinges and stood back to let them see.

Solomon and his dad both gasped. Sitting on the back of a lorry was the most amazing machine they had ever seen. At one end was a long funnel with a pair of bellows attached. This led to a big copper chamber with see-through pipes going in and out of it. Underneath the chamber a trapdoor opened onto a chute which led down to a conveyor belt, above which were suspended twenty hairdryers, a large pair of cattle-branders and a stapler. At the side was a big red On/Off lever. It was in the Off position.

"What does it do?" asked Solomon.

"Aha," said Mr Bunce. "I knew you'd like it, young man. First you fill a bowl with the sorts of things monkeys like to eat and place it at the bottom of the funnel. Then, when you've lured them, hey presto! The bellows suck them up the funnel into the cleansing chamber, where they are dipped in sanitizing fluid. Then they fall out of the trapdoor, down the chute and onto the conveyor belt, where they are blow-dried, stamped with a personal number then packed in tea crates for easy transportation."

It sounded so simple. Could it really be the answer? There was only one way to find out.

"Come on," said Mr Smee, "there's no time to waste." Which there wasn't. Because whether they liked it or not, those monkeys needed dealing with – and dealing with fast.

They climbed into the front of the lorry and drove out of the shed, taking much of it with them as they went. They ploughed across Mr Bunce's back garden, through a hedge at the side and onto the road. "Yee-hah!" cried Solomon. Mr Smee shut his eyes and was jolly glad that Mr Bunce had at least installed seatbelts.

In the courtyard of the Municipal Offices the scene was one of utter chaos. The monkeys were all hanging out of the windows hurling abuse and office stationery.

But just as the monkeys were about to start on a new batch of special Municipal embossed pencils, Mr Smee, Solomon and Mr Bunce hurtled into the courtyard aboard the incredible invention. "Out of the way!" shouted Mr Bunce, waving his arms out of the window. Everyone did as they were told and moved as far back as they could without falling into the ornamental newt pond. The monkeys dropped their pencils and peered with interest as the machine came to a squealing halt amid a cloud of exhaust.

"What is it?" asked one protestor.

"What does it do?" asked another.

"Hoop," said the monkeys.

"Ladies and Gentleman," said Terry Bunce, bowing to the crowd. "This is the Amazing Automatic Monkey-Catching Machine. And with it I will rid Royal Nerdal Norton of these unsavoury creatures that have terrorized all of us with their poor manners and habit of breaking things."

The crowd cheered. Solomon crossed his fingers.

"What happens first?" asked Mr Smee.

"First I need tasty items to lure the monkeys. Everyone search your pockets," he said to the crowd.

130

"I have three marshmallows and a fig," said Mr Ganges.

"I have a packet of chocolate-covered ants, which have melted a bit," said Mr Bottleopener. "They're most useful as a remedy for trapped wind," he added to no one in particular.

"I have a packet of turnip flavoured crisps," said Manjit the postman.

"We have Black Forest gâteau flavoured popsicles," said Doreen and Maureen, showing off loudly.

"Super," said Mr Bunce, holding out a bowl into which they threw their food. "This will do nicely."

He placed the bowl at the bottom of the enormous funnel.

"Now everyone must move back so the monkeys can see the bait." And he shooed everyone back again to the ornamental newt pond.

"Now we have to wait," he said.

"How long?" asked Solomon impatiently.

"Oh, a couple of minutes tops," said Mr Bunce.

He was right. The monkeys were far too fascinated by the machine and the bowl of snacks to stay inside the Municipal Offices for long. One by one they clambered out of the windows, scaling down drainpipes and vines until all sixty-seven small monkeys and the ten fearsome langurs were assembled in front of the machine.

"Wait a minute ... wait a minute..." said Mr Bunce softly, with one hand on the On/Off lever.

Then a small monkey sniffed the snacks and put his paw out to pick up Mr Ganges' big fig. Mr Bunce yanked down on the lever hard. It was fantastic. A hundred fairy lights lit up like the Blackpool Illuminations (which of course no one in Royal Nerdal Norton had ever heard of, but they still thought it looked super). Puffs of smoke came out of a small chimney at the top. Cogs turned, handles whizzed and the whole machine clanked, whirred and chugged.

But it was what happened to the monkeys that was the most amazing sight of all. Because as each monkey came up to the bowl of food, the enormous bellows squeezed, and up shot the monkey inside a transparent tube shaped like a helter-skelter before disappearing inside the barrel. One after another they whizzed up on their hairy backsides, shrieking very loudly as they went, until all seventy-seven had disappeared.

"Hurray!" shouted the crowd.

But something wasn't quite right.

"Aren't they supposed to be coming out all shiny and fresh onto the conveyor, ready for their blow-dry before being packed into tea crates?" asked Mr Smee.

"Hmm, well, yes," said Mr Bunce.

"Didn't you test it?" asked Solomon.

"Yes, but only on my cat Kevin," said Mr Bunce. "I don't have a hoard of marauding monkeys on hand just for trial runs, you know."

While Mr Bunce's Amazing Automatic Monkey-Catching Machine was indeed a feat of technical wizardry, it was only designed to cope with a small number of relatively well-behaved animals. Finding itself suddenly full of hooping, scratching bundles of fur and claws it panicked and went into emergency mode. The lights went off and the machine made a very loud grinding noise.

"Now what's it doing?" said Solomon, hopping from one foot to another in panic.

But before Mr Bunce could even think of an answer, the machine belched loudly, then *blam!* Out shot a wet and bedraggled monkey from the overflow chute on the top.

"Crikey!" said Solomon.

Kerpow! Another monkey flew over the heads of the crowd, hooping loudly as it spun.

Instead of stamping them and boxing them up, the machine was sending them all out the reject exit.

Wham! Out shot an enormous langur, landing on Mr Jambutty's ice-cream cart, which had only just been repaired by Mr Ganges.

The sky was full of whirling primates.

"Wheeee!" called the crowd as another monkey soared past in a graceful arc.

But it didn't stop there.

The Mayor, who had been sheltering in the Municipal Wine and Cheese Cellar, came stomping across the courtyard followed by his servant Minoo, and stood right next to the bowl of leftover snacks with his hands on his hips.

"I wouldn't go too near there if I were you, sir!" said Mr Smee.

"Don't you tell me what to do, you—" retorted the Mayor, who was not in the mood for being told anything at all unless it involved monkeys being captured. "I shall go where I jolly well like."

134

"But sir!" pleaded Mr Smee.

But it was too late. The machine, thinking an enormous gorilla had stepped into the trap, heaved an enormous heave on the bellows and sucked the Mayor up the whirly tube.

"Oooh," gasped the crowd.

"Mayor Plusfour!" said Minoo. "You must be getting out of there at once I think!" But the Mayor could not hear. He whirled around and around towards the cleansing chamber before becoming wedged upside down in a U-bend.

"Oh my goodness," said Mr Smee. "Mayor Plusfour is stuck! What shall we do?"

"There's nothing we can do," said Mr Bunce. "It's up to the machine now."

"Oh I don't think he will like that very much," said Minoo worriedly. "He has a golfing fixture with Mr Limpopo and Mr Limpopo this afternoon."

But he needn't have worried. The machine gave a last enormous heave on the bellows and the Mayor shot headfirst into the copper chamber.

Mr Smee shook his head. "Now what?" he said to Mr Bunce. But Mr Bunce didn't hear him. Like everyone else he was staring at the Amazing

Machine, wondering what other tricks it had up its sleeves – or rather, funnels. He didn't have to wonder long. The trapdoor under the copper chamber opened, and a dripping wet Mayor dropped down the chute and onto the conveyor belt, which started moving slowly.

"Smee! I'll have your guts for—" blustered the Mayor, but his words were drowned out by the sound of twenty hairdryers on full speed, blow-drying the Mayor's hair and moustache into enormous puffballs. "Aaaagh!" he cried. But the hairdryers were not the worst of it. As he rolled along the conveyor the cattle branders came plunging down and stamped a "1" on his forehead in red ink. "Hell and hot-water bottles!" he said. But the machine took no notice and picked him up with a giant pair of tweezers, dropped him in a packing crate, stapled the lid shut and deposited him ready for shipping in front of Mr Smee and Solomon.

"Oh dear," said Mr Smee.

"Oh dear indeed," said the crate. "This is it. You have gone one step too far, Smee. You are a nitwit, a halfwit and a dimwit besides. You are the most useless Municipal Complaints Clerk I have ever employed – and believe me, some of the others have been pretty hopeless. Now pack your bags and say your goodbyes. Because tomorrow morning you are going to be sent into the Forest of Certain Death to look for lost golf balls. And as for Solomon, this is the last idea he'll ever have. He will be sent to Barry Chatterjee's Home for Unruly Youth in the morning, where he will be tied up with parcel string so he can't cause any more damage."

"But what about the monkeys?" asked Solomon in a faint voice.

"I am going to get a huge gun and shoot every last one of their hairy backsides."

"But you can't!" said Solomon. "That's against the law."

"Then I'll change it!" thundered the Mayor.

Mr Smee and Solomon walked home slowly. All in all, it had not been a good week.

Solomon Sneaks Out

"Maybe the Mayor is right," said Mr Smee as they sat at home that evening. "Maybe I am a hopeless nit-wit. Maybe you'd be better off without me, Solomon."

"You're not a nitwit, Dad," said Solomon. "You just haven't found the right answer to the complaint yet."

"Yes he is," said Aunt Nehemiah meanly. "In my day, when anything needed fixing we called up a freelance Russian pirate called Boris Kalashnikov, who pulled people's nails out with industrial pliers and then grated the soles of his victims' feet with a big cheese grater until they begged to be locked up."

"And where would I find such a ghastly individual?" asked Mr Smee wearily.

"In the phone book under 'B' for bandit," replied Aunt Nehemiah. "Or maybe 'E' for evil."

For the second time that day Mr Smee pulled the phone book off the shelf and flicked through furiously. "Back specialists, bag-makers, band uniform designers, bandy-legged flamingos..." he read. "But no bandits! And there are no mercenaries, pirates, villains, fiends or bearded baddies, either." And he slammed the phone book shut. "This is ridiculous. I'm going to lose my job in the morning and will have to go to the Forest of Certain Death and find golf balls until I die, which will almost certainly be very quickly."

"And you'll never marry Lysandra, either," added Solomon gloomily.

"Marry Lysandra?" snapped Aunt Nehemiah. "Hah, you have more hope of marrying the Queen of Sheba."

Mr Smee put his head in his hands and sobbed.

"Now look what you've done, Solomon," screeched Aunt Nehemiah. "Go to your room this instant!"

Solomon stamped up the stairs and sat on the edge of his wooden bed. He was angry. He was angry with the Mayor for threatening everyone. He was angry with Aunt Nehemiah for being so mean. But most of all he was angry with himself for not thinking of a way to help his dad. A fat tear rolled down his cheek and plopped onto the floor.

Solomon thought about everything that had happened over the last week. The funny thing was, he had enjoyed it. What's more, he rather liked the monkeys as well – they were enormous fun, and certainly the most interesting thing to have happened to Royal Nerdal Norton for a long, long time. There just had to be a way of catching them safely before the Mayor got out his big shotgun. But he had tried all his books and, while he had learnt that the name for a group of crows was a "murder" and that polar-bear liver was poisonous, he had not found a single way to catch a monkey.

The town library had been out of bounds since the monkeys had restacked everything in the wrong order. Mr Armitage the librarian was working overtime removing slightly racy romances from the under-5s' Look and Learn section. And school was closed for the summer, so he couldn't use the library there.

But wait a minute! Solomon thought hard. Hadn't his dad said the Mayor had a library?

"That's it!" Solomon whispered to himself in bed. "The Mayor's house." But he had to get there fast, because by tomorrow morning the Mayor would have polished up his pistol for some monkey hunting. Solomon pulled off his yellow candlewick cover and slid out of bed. Then, as silent as could be, he put on some trousers and a T-shirt and a pair of sandals. Then came the tricky part. He could hardly trot downstairs and announce to his dad and Aunt Nehemiah that he was going to the Mayor's house to break into the library. There was only one thing for it. He would have to climb out of the window and down the fire escape.

He pushed a pillow under his bedcover quickly so that if anyone came to check on him it would look like he was fast asleep. Then he clambered onto the windowsill and lowered himself down backwards. The steps were further down than he thought and even when he was just holding on with his fingertips his toes couldn't quite reach. He would have to let go and hope for the best. He counted to three. Then he counted to three again to be sure, and let go. *Clank!* went the fire escape. "Hellfire," whispered Solomon.

"What was that?" said Aunt Nehemiah, who was sitting on the sofa reading *100 Ways with a Pig's Trotter*.

Mr Smee looked up wearily. He was still upset. "I didn't hear anything," he said.

"Yes, well, you'd better be right," said Aunt Nehemiah. "I do not want any more excrement on any of my extremities."

But Mr Smee was too miserable to listen.

Solomon watched through the window until Aunt Nehemiah looked back down at her book again. Then, faster than you can say "red lorry, yellow lorry", he was off and running down the road in the hot dark night, past the Barry Chatterjee Centre for Unruly Youth, past the Arthur Gomez Memorial Bandstand, past the Municipal Offices, where the monkeys lay sleeping off the day's excitement, off towards the right side of Royal Nerdal Norton and the Mayor's mansion.

Lysandra and Solomon Hatch a Plan

Solomon looked up at the house, with its pink pillars and ornamental gardens. There was no mistaking it, it stood out like an iced fairy cake. But Solomon had overlooked one thing. He had no idea where the library was. How could I have been so stupid? he thought to himself. He counted the windows. There were thirty-six on the front of the house alone. The chances of his picking the right one were not very high. And anyway, he didn't want to have to break any glass – that was vandalism, and he was in enough trouble already. He would just have to hope that one window, somewhere in the mansion, had been left open. Then he would have to search every room in the house until he found the library. And he had better get started pronto because time was not on his side.

Solomon walked slowly round the house, hiding

behind the bushes as he went. I hope they don't keep tigers or other ferocious animals, he thought to himself, his heart beating so loudly he was sure someone would hear it. Window after window was shut. How do they bear the heat? thought Solomon. But then he decided the Mayor probably had top-of-the-range air-conditioning installed. Which he did.

But, at the top of the mansion, one room did not have air-conditioning. And do you know why? Because it is bad for books.

The window in the library was the only one that was ever opened – so that whoever needed to read the books or newspapers wouldn't wilt in the heat. So right up at the top of the mansion a turret window sat temptingly open, winking at Solomon in the night, beckoning him inside. But there was one problem.

"Oh lawks," Solomon said to himself. "That's rather high up." But then he thought of the alternative. His dad would lose his job and have to go to the Forest of Certain Death, the poor monkeys would get their backsides (and maybe worse) filled with lead shot from the Mayor's own blunderbuss and he would be tied up with parcel string by Barry Chatterjee. Then Solomon spotted a drainpipe in a rather convenient place, and it was true to say he was a champion climber in PE at school. He could shin up and down a rope or pole faster than any other boy or girl. So before he knew it, Solomon had talked himself into climbing. He jumped up in the air to grab the iron drainpipe with both hands and then brought his knees up as high as he could. Then, gripping with his sandals, he pushed up again and grabbed higher. It wasn't too hard. As long as he didn't look down. But Solomon had his eyes tight shut, so he couldn't look down even if he wanted to. He knew that the best thing would be to climb until he could feel the gutter above him. Which all of a sudden he did, with an almighty clonk on the top of his head. "Ow!" he yelped, then cursed himself silently for making a noise.

But it was too late. Behind the window something stirred. "Who's out there?" said a voice. Solomon, who was crouching on the windowsill, held his breath and shut his eyes again. Please go away, he thought to himself. Please, please don't see me.

But the owner of the voice was not going to go away. Instead they came to the window and stared straight at Solomon.

"Harry?" said the voice. "It can't be."

Solomon, who was slightly confused, opened his eyes. Framed in the light of the window was the most beautiful woman he had ever seen. She had hair the colour of spun gold and eyes like sapphires. No one could possibly be that lovely. Then he realized who it must be. "Lysandra," he whispered.

"Yes," she smiled. "I am Lysandra. But you ... you look like ... but you couldn't be. But the same eyes, the glasses, the same dark, dark hair..."

Solomon knew what she was thinking. "My father," he said. "Harry is my father. I'm Solomon Smee."

Lysandra smiled at Solomon, then hugged him and pulled him inside and sobbed and laughed all at once. A monkey's wedding, thought Solomon. Rainy and sunny at the same time. And he hugged her back. His father was right, she was kind and wonderful and he felt happier than he had in a long time.

"But what are you doing here?" asked Lysandra.

"Does your dad know where you are?"

Solomon shook his head. "My father needs help," he said. "Monkeys are on the rampage in Royal Nerdal Norton, and if Dad doesn't catch them by tomorrow then he'll be sent to the Forest of Certain Death, where he'll die."

"Certainly," said Lysandra.

"And I'll be sent to Barry Chatterjee's Centre for Unruly Youth even though I am not at all unruly and eat all my dinner even when it's brains and can do the twelve times table. And worst of all the Mayor will get out his big shotgun and shoot the monkeys even though it's illegal but he says he will change the law and I've looked in my dictionary and comics but there's nothing in there except that a 'monkey jacket' is also called a 'mess jacket' and so I came here because of the library and..."

"Slow down!" said Lysandra, exhausted at Solomon's blurting everything out. "Now. Let's think about this. I know your father has tried the army and Maurice Hankey and bigger monkeys, and I know that the Amazing Automatic Monkey-Catching Machine only managed to catch the Mayor – which I thought was rather funny," added Lysandra, laughing.

"But how do you know about all that?" Solomon asked. "I thought you never went out."

"I don't," said Lysandra. "But the world comes to me." And she pointed at her leather box, which was open on the table. "Go on," she said, "look inside."

Solomon frowned and peered in. Inside were piles of newspaper cuttings.

"Oh," he said. "I see."

"But you don't. Not quite," said Lysandra. "Whenever I read the newspapers I cut out anything interesting. Sometimes stories of bandits. Sometimes just a face I like. Sometimes stories of my old friends from long ago – like your father. But there are also tales from far away, of dastardly plots foiled by secret agents, of shipwrecks and daring adventures on desert islands."

Solomon wasn't at all sure where this was going. "But Lysandra," he ventured.

"No, wait," she said, sensing his impatience. "The thing is, I remember a story from four or five years ago. It was the tale of a man who caught a monkey in a grand palace and thwarted the biggest diamond heist of all time. And I know I cut that story out, and if we could just find it and find out how that man caught the monkey we could use the same trick ourselves."

Solomon turned to Lysandra with a desperate look in his eyes. "There's not much time," he said.

"Then we'll start at once," said Lysandra, tipping up the leather box and spilling the yellowing cuttings out onto the table. "You start at that end of the table and I'll take this end and we'll meet in the middle."

"OK," said Solomon determinedly. "Let's go!"

And so together, behind the high-up window in the turret, with the light burning bright into the hot night, Solomon and Lysandra read the papers.

Monkey Onassis and the Mirash Diamond

An hour later and they had gone through a hundred articles each. They had read the news of the great drought of thirteen years ago when everyone had to drink bottled lemonade to survive, even the animals. They had read the story of Dread Pirate Dick and his crew of one-eyed shipmates who stole the gold from the vaults in Xanadu and were last seen sailing wonkily into the sunset, what with them all only having one eye. They had even read the tragic tale of when Lysandra's own mother disappeared in the Lux cinema in a puff of smoke and a smell like burnt pilchards.

Until finally, just before the grandfather clock in the hallway struck one in the morning, Solomon picked up a small scrap of paper from the middle of the pile and wearily read the headline. Then he read it again, to be sure. It was – it really was it.

"Lysandra," he said.

"Mmm?" she said, her eyes almost shut.

"I think I have it."

Lysandra opened her eyes. "Really?"

"Really," said Solomon. "Listen." And he read out the story of exactly how the great Gaston Regis d'Angin Cummerbund had caught the world-famous diamond thief Monkey Onassis before he escaped from the Doge's palace with the priceless Mirash Diamond wedged in his hairy fist.

"Do you think it'll work?" said Solomon, his eyes as big as saucers.

"I do. Of course I do!" said Lysandra, and she hugged Solomon tight. "Now come on, we have to tell your father."

Solomon laughed as she swung him round in the air.

"But we'll go out the front door this time," added Lysandra. "I don't think I can still get down the drainpipe."

"You mean you did once?" asked Solomon.

"Of course," said Lysandra. "When I was a little girl."

Solomon was wide-eyed. She truly was fantastic.

And so, with the newspaper cutting in his pocket and his hand firmly in Lysandra's, Solomon tiptoed down the darkened hallways of the Mayor's mansion, past the crystal chandeliers, past the brass doorknobs, past the tiger's head on a wooden plaque which said "Cowpatty Province, August 1893" and out of the wide front door towards the wrong side of town.

The Plan

M_r Smee, who had fallen asleep on the sofa still sorrowfully pondering his future, awoke with a start. Then he promptly decided it was one of those dreams where you think you've woken up but actually you're still asleep. So he ignored what he had seen and turned over.

But the dream was very persistent and shook him again. "Harry," it said. "Wake up."

He opened one eye.

"Hello, Harry," said the dream. "I expect this is a bit of a shock." Then a smaller being, which looked remarkably like his son Solomon, loomed into view waving a piece of paper at him.

"Dad, for heaven's sake get up."

Then Mr Smee realized it wasn't a dream. His heart gave a small leap as he rubbed his eyes in amazement. "Lysandra?" he said.

"Yes, it's me." Lysandra smiled at him.

"But what ... and how ... and why ... and shouldn't you be in bed, Solomon?" said Mr Smee.

"Don't be angry with him, Harry. He did this for you," said Lysandra.

Mr Smee stared at her. He couldn't believe his eyes. She was more beautiful than he remembered.

"My Lysandra," he said softly, his eyes almost brimming over. "I thought I had lost you for ever." He reached out to touch her hand.

Solomon sighed. "Oh yuck, for heaven's sake there's no time for that malarkey. She's here because we have the answer to the monkey menace."

Lysandra nodded. "He's right, Harry. You and I and Solomon are going to catch the monkeys tonight."

"Really?" said Mr Smee, coming down to earth with a bang. "But how do you propose to achieve the thing that has evaded a court magician, the army and a top-class inventor, not to mention your own father?"

"Coconuts and satsumas," said Solomon.

"Pardon?" said Mr Smee.

"Coconuts and satsumas," said Lysandra.

Mr Smee thought for a second. He had nothing

to lose. And, it had to be said, everything to gain now that Lysandra was here. "OK," he said. "How does it work?"

"Right," said Solomon. "Here goes. What you do is cut open a large coconut. Then you peel a satsuma, pop it inside the coconut and seal the whole caboodle up again. But in the lid of the nut you drill a hole, just big enough for a hairy monkey arm. Then you hide and wait. When the monkey comes along and smells the satsuma he can't resist putting his arm inside the nut, but when he tries to pull it out again, the satsuma is too big to go through the hole and he is trapped."

"But why don't they just let go of the satsuma?" asked Mr Smee.

"Because monkeys are very greedy and very silly and they won't let go," said Lysandra.

"Are you sure about this?" said Mr Smee.

"Look – it's in the newspaper, see." Solomon handed him the cutting.

"Mmm-hmm," said Mr Smee, reading to himself. "Monkey Onassis. Mirash. Hmm." And he put the cutting down on the arm of the sofa. "Well I suppose it can't be any worse than fishing-rods and

French fancies. But there's one problem."

"What?" asked Solomon and Lysandra.

"It's too late," said Mr Smee. "I'm being demoted first thing in the morning and the greengrocers' are all shut now. We can't do it."

"Nonsense," said Lysandra. "There's no such thing as can't – only won't or don't want to. We'll pick the coconuts and satsumas from the fruit groves and drill them ourselves, even if it takes all night."

"You're crazy!" said Mr Smee.

Lysandra laughed. "Come on, Harry," she said. "It'll be just like old times."

"Let's do it!" cried Solomon.

"Do what?" snapped a voice from behind them. Solomon looked round. At the top of the stairs, in a black dressing gown and with her greasy hair in rollers, stood Aunt Nehemiah.

"Solomon Smee, I am talking to you. What are you doing up at this time and what is it that you think you are going to do?" she said, stomping down the stairs.

"Er... Um..." stuttered Solomon.

"We're going to catch the monkeys, madam," said Lysandra politely.

"Oh are you?" said Aunt Nehemiah. "And who exactly might you be, and what are you doing in my house at two o'clock in the morning?"

"This is Lysandra. My oldest friend," said Mr Smee. "And she is here in My house as My guest," he added boldly.

Aunt Nehemiah flashed her black eyes at him. Even in the half-light Solomon could see that the hair on her wart stood out electrically. That was bad news.

"And just how do you three think you are going to catch seventy-seven monkeys?" she demanded.

"With coconuts and satsumas," said Lysandra.

Aunt Nehemiah could not believe her ears.

"Is she mad?" she said to Mr Smee. "Maybe that is why she has been locked up. In my day, all mad people were kept in dungeons so that no one had to listen to their rantings."

"That's not a bad idea," said Mr Smee quietly.

"What?" said Aunt Nehemiah.

"Nothing," said Mr Smee.

Solomon nudged him. He couldn't let Aunt Nehemiah stop them now.

Mr Smee took the hint. "Now listen to me,

Nehemiah," he said. "The fact is, we're jolly well going to try this thing out because it's our only hope. Come on, Lysandra, and you too, Solomon. We had better be off."

Solomon smiled at his dad and held onto his hand as they walked out of the door behind Lysandra, leaving Aunt Nehemiah speechless in her dressing gown and rollers.

Coconuts and Satsumas

M_r Smee, Lysandra and Solomon set off to the fruit grove on the edge of Royal Nerdal Norton. They walked and walked through the wrong side of town, past the small wooden houses shuttered up for the night, past the Municipal rubbish dump with its piles of broken bicycle bits and pram wheels, until they reached the swampy banks of the river Nerdal, which was usually a wide brown dawdling thing but had dried to a small trickle and a lot of sludge. But the river was not what they had come to see. What they wanted was high above their heads: the hundreds of green coconuts clumped on the trunks of the coconut trees.

"How do we get them down?" asked Solomon. It was an awfully long way up and they had not brought a ladder with them – only a net, a saw to cut up the coconuts, some glue, a drill to make the holes and his small red cart to carry everything on.

"Well," said Lysandra, "one of us must shin up the trees and hit the coconuts with a stick until they fall down, and the other two can catch them at the bottom with the net."

"I'll do it," said Mr Smee.

"Are you sure, Dad?" said Solomon. "I can climb, you know – I'm really very good."

Mr Smee shook his head. "No, this is something I want to do."

Lysandra smiled. "You can do it, Harry. You always were the best climber."

"OK," he said, blushing. "Here I go." And with a stick pushed through his belt he put his arms around the knobbly papery trunk of the tree and started climbing.

Gosh it was hard. Mr Smee had forgotten just how tricky it could be. But he had to show Lysandra and Solomon that he was made of tougher stuff. Aunt Nehemiah had just been the start. He was going to be a new man. No one was going to put him down any more, no one.

But it was a long time since he had climbed so high, and soon he was out of puff and sweaty in the summer heat. He looked down. Solomon and Lysandra looked very small and far away. He started to feel dizzy.

"That's it," said Lysandra. "You're nearly there. Don't stop now. Just a bit further to go."

"I feel sick," said Mr Smee, his head swimming.

"Don't look down," said Lysandra.

"Keep your eyes on the nuts," said Solomon.

Mr Smee took some long breaths and set off again. Lysandra was right, it wasn't too far, and he soon reached the clusters of enormous coconuts.

"Right," said Lysandra. "Now comes the tricky bit. You must let go with one hand and grab hold of the hitting stick."

Mr Smee shut his eyes and tried. But his hand was frozen to the spot. "I can't," he cried. "I can't move."

"Yes you can," said Lysandra. "Come on. The trick is to forget how high up you are. Imagine you're just standing on the kitchen floor and reaching up to swat a fly that's annoying you. Or imagine someone you really hate shouting in your face, and hit them with a tennis racquet – *bam!* – on the top of their head."

Mr Smee thought. He thought about the kitchen

at home and a big fruit fly sitting on the apricots on the top shelf. But he still felt funny. So he thought about the Mayor and his big red face and long waxed moustache, shouting and stomping and threatening to demote him.

And then something incredible happened. He stopped feeling sick. Instead he felt angry. Very angry indeed. And he grabbed the stick from his belt and he hit those coconuts with such a thwack that three went flying down towards Lysandra and Solomon at once.

Solomon whooped with excitement. "That's it, Dad!" he cried as he hopped one way and then another with his net to catch the falling nuts. "Keep going!"

And Mr Smee did. He hit those coconuts until seventy-seven of them had plopped into the net and were stacked on the little red cart.

"Hurrah!" shouted Lysandra. "You've done it, Harry. Bravo! Now you can come down."

Mr Smee smiled. He could hardly believe it. He was so happy he forgot how high he was and shinned down the tree in one minute flat.

"Well done," said Lysandra when he got to the

bottom. "I knew you could do it." And she gave him a hug.

Solomon groaned. "Come on," he said. "We can't shilly-shally. We still have satsumas to pluck."

So the trio set off with their little red cart along the river to the satsuma patch.

As everyone knows, satsuma trees are very small, so they picked the little orange fruits and in no time at all they had enough to fill the nuts and a few more to eat as well.

"We can saw them all up here," said Mr Smee. "If we do it at the Municipal Offices then we might wake the monkeys, and then who knows what would happen?"

"Good idea," said Lysandra.

"Right, let's form a line. I'll saw, Solomon can pop in the satsumas, and Lysandra, you can be in charge of glueing. Then I'll run to the other end and drill the holes in the tops."

And that's exactly what they did. They cut open seventy-seven coconuts, poured out the sweet watery milk from inside and then dropped a satsuma into each of them. Then they sealed them up with cow gum before drilling a hole in the top, just big enough for a hairy monkey arm to fit in.

"But what about the langurs?" asked Solomon. "Their arms are fatter and furrier."

"Oh I'm quite sure they'll be able to fit at least their fingers inside," said Lysandra. "Where there's food involved monkeys will jam their hands in any small crevice or crack."

Then Solomon thought about a question that had been bothering him, and decided now was a good time to ask.

"Why do you think the monkeys came here, Lysandra? What do they want with us?" he said.

"Well, Solomon," she said. "I've been thinking about this, and I may just have the answer. The monkeys of Royal Nerdal Norton lived for many years in the mangosteen trees on the edge of the town, occupying themselves with fruit and insects and the river. Sometimes they would take an outing to the Municipal rubbish dump to play with old bicycle wheels and broken fridges. But mainly they kept out of the way of the humans. Until one day the Municipal Council decided to build a bypass right through their homes. Diggers and rollers and men with clipboards arrived and knocked down the mangosteen trees and laid a big wide tarmac road where once had been lush grass and fruit.

"The homeless monkeys sat at the edge of the roadside and watched forlornly as the brightly coloured bus drove past, crammed with people in fantastic hats. They saw Manjit the postman whizz along on his racing bicycle. They saw the Municipal brass band in their maroon-and-gold uniforms sail by on a carnival float playing calypso music. They saw scooters and roller skates and an ice-cream cart. And after a while they decided they wanted to teach these people a lesson. So one hot night they set off from the rubbish dump towards the glowing lights of Royal Nerdal Norton. They crept softly down the dusty tarmac road until they reached the edge of town. Then they stopped and sniffed the wind and made a noise that sounded like 'hoop' and which meant that they were very excited.

"They walked past the Barry Chatterjee Centre for Unruly Youth, where forty naughty boys were sleeping in bunk beds in stripy pyjamas and dreaming of catapults and cigars and tattoos. They walked past the Arthur Gomez Memorial Bandstand where rows of gold chairs sat empty, past the great, grey Limpopo and Limpopo department store, until they saw what they were looking for."

"What was that?" asked Solomon.

"Mischief, of course," said Lysandra. "Now come on, we mustn't waste any more time. There's still work to be done."

And so pulling the little red cart behind him, Solomon followed Lysandra and Mr Smee as they crept back into town, past the small house where Aunt Nehemiah lay snoring angrily, past the Barry Chatterjee Centre for Unruly Youth, past the Arthur Gomez Memorial Bandstand and up to the grounds of the Municipal Offices, where the monkeys were asleep in a magnolia tree.

Tiptoeing so as not to wake them, they carefully unloaded their loot, setting the coconuts on the ground beneath the branches. Then, exhausted by the night's work they all fell fast asleep on top of the cart.

A New Beginning

"Thump, thump, hoop," went the noise.

Solomon turned over on the cart for forty more winks.

But then he heard it again. "Thump, thump, hoop!"

And again.

He nudged Lysandra.

"Wake up!" he said.

Lysandra stretched out. "What is it, Solomon?" she asked sleepily.

Then she saw it. "Oh my goodness!" And she nudged Mr Smee.

Mr Smee opened one eye. "What's wrong?"

"Nothing's wrong," said Lysandra. "In fact, everything's right. I think we've done it."

Mr Smee sat bolt upright on the cart and looked around him. He smiled.

"By Jove," he said. "We jolly well have done it."

And they had. Because surrounding the little red cart were seventy-seven monkeys, all with their hands or fingers jammed inside coconuts, which they were banging on the ground to try to get off, hooping very loudly because it wasn't working.

"Solomon, my boy, you are a genius!" said Mr Smee. "And you too, Lysandra. You may have saved both our lives and the monkeys' as well."

"No, I should be thanking you," said Lysandra. "You have saved me as well. From a life wasted inside. From now on I'm going to do as I please."

"Me too," said Mr Smee.

"Me too," said Solomon.

Mr Smee laughed. "I don't think so, young man. Not quite yet, anyway."

"Listen, Solomon," said Lysandra. "There's still one more thing to be done. I need you to run to my house and fetch my father at once."

"Of course," said Solomon happily.

"And get your Aunt Nehemiah as well – it's about time she knew how clever you are," added Mr Smee.

"OK, Dad." And Solomon ran as fast as he could in the morning sun towards the pink fairy cake mansion.

Minoo answered the door in his stripy pyjamas. "Hello, Solomon," he said. "What is the catastrophe that means I have to wake the Mayor up at this early hour and get a double shouting-at for my trouble?"

"It's the monkeys," said Solomon, panting with all the running he'd done. "We've caught them."

"What, all of them?" asked Minoo.

"Every last furry one of them," said Solomon, laughing. "Me and my dad and Lysandra."

"Lysandra? Are you sure? But she isn't allowed out of the house, let alone to gallivant with monkeys. I tell you, young Solomon, the Mayor will be most aggravated."

"Not when he sees what we've done," laughed Solomon, and waving to Minoo he ran back to town.

When he got to his own wooden house he shouted up at the window, "Aunt Nehemiah! Aunt Nehemiah, wake up!"

He didn't have to wait long. The window swung open and a particularly nasty-looking Aunt Nehemiah appeared with a black hat and an even blacker look.

"In my day children knocked politely then waited

in the rain and snow for someone to let them in even if it took five days," she snapped.

"Never mind in your day, Aunt Nehemiah. In my day children can shout sometimes if they like. And anyway, you won't care when you see what we've done," cried Solomon.

"Well we'll see about that, young man. Because if you're messing around again it'll be four smacks with a wet slipper and bed in the coal cellar." And she slammed the window shut.

Back in the gardens of the Municipal Offices a crowd was already gathering. First to arrive was Mr Ganges the garage mechanic, who had heard the banging all the way from the Almighty Honk Car Repair and Accessories Centre. He was closely followed by Mrs Perambulator and her spoilt daughters Maureen and Doreen, who had seen Mr Ganges run past and did not want to miss out on any gossip. Then came Mr Bottleopener the chemist, the Limpopos senior and junior, Mr Jambutty the out-of-work ice-cream man, Mrs Britt-Dullforce, who had abandoned the picket line because the monkeys kept stealing her sleeping bag, Manjit the postman, Maurice Hankey,

Aunt Nehemiah, Boyce Spink and, finally, the Mayor, pulled by Minoo in a rickshaw.

"You'd better not be telling fibs," said the Mayor to Solomon as he squeezed out of the rickshaw. "You know I do not like being woken up unless bandits are invading or there is an extra-special breakfast waiting for me downstairs."

"I'm not," said Solomon. "Look around."

The Mayor looked around. Then he looked again because he hadn't believed it the first time. The crowd looked around too. There they were – sixty-seven small monkeys and ten fearsome langurs all looking glumly at the coconuts stuck on their hairy hands.

"Well bless my soul," said Mr Ganges.

"Coo," said the Perambulator twins.

"Golly," said Mr Jambutty.

"But how and when and what with?" stuttered the Mayor. "And what on earth are you doing here, Lysandra?" he demanded, noticing his daughter for the first time.

"I'm here to help my friends, Harry and Solomon," said Lysandra. "They caught the monkeys themselves without magicians or the army or amazing machinery.

Just wit and cunning and plain cleverness."

"But..." spluttered the Mayor.

"No buts, Dad," said Lysandra.

The Mayor glowered, although he was secretly so glad the monkeys were caught that he would have forgiven Lysandra anything. "Well that's all very nice," he said, "but what do we do with them now, eh? Didn't think about that, did you?"

"Exactly," said Maurice, crossing his arms, slightly annoyed that they had managed to catch the monkeys without any help from him.

"A monkey circus act!" said Mr Ganges. "I've seen them on telly. Put them in cowboy hats on those undersized Falabella ponies and we could make a fortune."

"Lock them up," said Mrs Perambulator. "I hear that in some Northern lands they have monkey prisons. Why, in Perratootoo they have eleven locked up for felons ranging from robbery to impersonating a police officer."

"No and No again!" shrieked Mrs Britt-Dullforce.

"No," agreed Lysandra. "You don't need a prison or a cowboy monkey act. You just need to give them what they want."

"And what might that be?" demanded the Mayor belligerently.

"A home, Dad," said Lysandra. "We knocked down their old one to build our bypass and now they have nowhere to go but the rubbish dump. What they need is somewhere with some trees and swings and slides and plenty of fruit, away from the road and away from the town."

"But that could take years to build," said the Mayor. "What do you propose to do with them in the meantime?"

"I've thought of that," said Lysandra. "Only one house in town has a big enough garden."

"But you're not suggesting..." said the Mayor.

"Yes I am," said Lysandra. "Until their new home is ready the monkeys can live with you."

"What a first-rate idea," said Mr Jambutty.

"Quite right," said Mr Ganges.

"How kind you are, Mayor!" said Mrs Perambulator.

The Mayor, sensing he could not turn his daughter down in public, could only agree. "Oh very well," he blustered. "But there is to be no ballyhoo, calamity or shenanigans – or weeing in the bath."

But then he thought harder. "Hang on a minute,

though," he said. "You said 'live with you'. Don't you mean the monkeys will come and live with 'us'?"

"He's right," said Solomon. "I think you got your sentence wrong."

"No I didn't," said Lysandra. "Because I'd like to marry Harry, Daddy, and move in with him and Solomon. That is – if he'll have me..."

Mr Smee's mouth dropped in amazement. "But ... of course!" he sputtered, and he hugged her so hard she came right off her feet.

"Now just wait one minute, Lysandra Plusfour," said the Mayor. "You let go of that man this instant and get back to your room."

"No," said Lysandra.

"What?" demanded the Mayor, yanking his moustache frenetically.

"You heard me, Dad. I'm sorry, but I'm thirty-four years old and quite old enough to make my own decisions – and you are fifty-seven and old enough to live without me."

"But ... but..." blustered the Mayor.

"No buts, Dad. I've made up my mind. I want to marry Harry. If that's OK with Solomon too, of course."

Solomon nodded happily.

"Well come on, then," said Mr Smee. "We'd better show you to your new home, Lysandra. But it's a little smaller than the mansion and not as pink, and the carpets are thin and there are just light bulbs instead of chandeliers."

"Stop!" cried Lysandra. "I'll love it no matter how small it is or how modest. It's not what the home looks like. It's who is in it."

Solomon reached up to hold her hand and she reached out to hold Mr Smee's, and together the three of them turned to leave.

"Just a minute, Smee," said the Mayor. "There's the small matter of your new job."

Mr Smee sighed; he knew it was all too good to be true. "Where to this time?" he asked. "The Department of Checking for Headlice on Small Schoolchildren, or perhaps the Office for Picking Those Annoying Balls of Fluff off Jumpers?"

"Not at all," said the Mayor. "In fact, I'm promoting you. As from now you are the Official Royal Nerdal Norton Monkey Monitor. You will get a new uniform and a bicycle and an extra week's holiday. Provided of course that the monkeys do as they're told."

"And an assistant," said Solomon. "He'll need one of those."

"Oh very well," said the Mayor. "That too. But only in the holidays."

Lysandra smiled at Mr Smee, who was lost for words, although that didn't matter because you can't do much talking when a big kiss is planted straight on your lips.

The crowd cheered and even the Mayor smiled, and Boyce Spink of the *Nerdal Norton Packet* pulled out a shiny new tape recorder ready to dictate tomorrow's headline and the next day's waste paper.

Epilogue

And so that is how Solomon Smee and his dad Harry won the battle against the monkeys – and the Mayor.

Now Mr Smee rides around town in a new uniform on a shiny bicycle checking for monkey business. Everyone claps and cheers when he goes past, and Mr Smee waves back.

Solomon still lives in the small house on the wrong side of town. But at night he sleeps happily in his wooden bed with the yellow candlewick cover. He never worries and is never ever bored, because now he has a new mum – Lysandra. She tells him fantastic stories, and lets him watch telly and eat jam and jelly as long as he cleans his teeth afterwards. The house is always bright and happy and there is cereal for breakfast instead of fish.

Best of all, Aunt Nehemiah has gone. She packed

her big black leather trunk the day the monkeys were captured and set off in search of a new job as a housekeeper. And she found one that afternoon – at Barry Chatterjee's Home for Unruly Youth, where she can shout at naughty boys to her heart's content.

And as for the Mayor and the monkeys... Well, he's got quite used to them being around. They sit happily together in the shade of the verandah and drink lemonade with fancy umbrellas in, and eat cake. Sometimes, if they are very good, the Mayor lets them watch television – as long as they sit quietly in rows and use the proper toilet. In fact, I think he will even miss them when they go.

Mrs Britt-Dullforce is in charge of complaints now. And they are back to the usual subjects. The heat, which is still making flip-flops melt and stick to the floor. Maurice Hankey, who is still turning people into goats. And noisy neighbours. Why, just yesterday Mr Ganges complained that Mrs Darjeeling at Number 23 was playing Johnny Sparkles' Greatest Hits at five in the morning.

And so apart from the occasional invasion by pirates from the North or bandits from the South,

Royal Nerdal Norton is back to its usual insignificant self. Still in the Kingdom of Elsewhere, just to the left of Nomansland and not far from Xanadu. And so small that only the gods, mapmakers, and now you, have heard of it.

MAISIE MORRIS AND THE AWFUL ARKWRIGHTS
Joanna Nadin

Maisie Morris lives with her mum in a titchy turret at the top of Withering Heights Retirement Home. While Mrs Morris looks after the residents, polishing bottoms and scrubbing smalls, Maisie plays cards and learns how to quickstep with the flamboyant Loveday Pink.

But they all live in fear of the odious owners, Mr and Mrs Arkwright, who serve cabbage water for lunch, confiscate pets and cancel Christmas. Maisie is convinced that nothing less than a miracle will deal with the revolting pair.

The great thing about miracles, though, is that you never know when one is lurking round the corner...